To all my family.

Not forgetting the furry, four-legged ones.

The Backwater

Judith Crow

Judith x

CROWVUS

First Published in 2018
Crowvus, 53 Argyle Square, Wick, KW1 5AJ

Copyright © Text Judith Crow 2018
Copyright © Cover Image Crowvus 2018

ISBN 978-0-9957860-5-9

www.crowvus.com

Rebecca Williams had known her mother was going to die. Six months to live, the all-too-familiar phrase that has been captured so many times in popular culture, had been the message from the doctor last Christmas.

There had only ever been Rebecca and her mother, so there were no secrets about what was going to happen. Her mum, headstrong as always, held on for nearly three months beyond the doctor's prediction and, in September, Rebecca found herself facing the funeral of the only relative she had ever known.

The final month had been the worst, she thought as she walked away from the crematorium with her mother's friends. Her mum had just been holding on, desperate not to leave her little girl and refusing to accept the inevitable. But they had enjoyed the spring together, especially the two weeks holiday paid for by anonymous well-wishers. Their trip had taken them to *Disneyland Paris* – a place her mother had promised to take her when she was younger, when financial constraints had made it impossible.

Afterwards, the council had provided a personal tutor for Rebecca so that she would not fall behind in her schooling. She knew that custody proceedings had been ongoing but had never taken the opportunity to discuss it with her mum. News of their continuing developments had been brought to the flat by a tight-lipped Social Worker. She had patted Rebecca's head patronisingly before sitting on the sofa beside her mother and talking in hushed tones of the continuing discussions regarding what would happen to the twelve-year-old.

Rebecca had acted, through the whole nightmarish chain of events, like she did not care about the custody fiasco. Friends and social workers would ask her who she would like to live with and she would just shrug her shoulders. The sole occasion when she almost allowed it to touch her was when her mother, by this point lying weakly in bed, had asked her.

"Who would you like to live with? If you could choose anyone in the world."

"Ed Sheeran," Rebecca had replied with a smile, before realising that her mum was serious. She had taken a deep breath and said, "I trust you to choose, Mum." Her mother's red eyes had welled with tears at this point and Rebecca had hastily changed the subject, something she had learnt to do during the long months of her mum's illness. Whenever it became too much for her, she would not walk away, she would just change the subject to try and block out the reality.

Rebecca was now officially in care, being looked after temporarily by her mother's friend, Judy, until the custody proceedings could be concluded. She knew that her mum had detailed her own preference, but she had no idea who it was. She looked out of the window, waiting for the tight-lipped Social Worker to appear and, sure enough, at quarter to five that afternoon, the woman pulled up in a red BMW, knocked on the door and waited to be allowed in.

This time, instead of ruffling Rebecca's hair, she sat down with her and Judy on the white sofa and spoke to her in a quiet, respectful way, which made Rebecca sit up and pay attention.

"The custody hearings have finished," she said with a tight smile. "You're going to live with your father in Lincolnshire. He's got a lovely house in the country."

"My father?" Rebecca asked. "Why?"

"It was your mother's request. Following discussions, the authorities are confident he will provide a good home for you."

Rebecca looked across at Judy, whose lips were pursed into a forced smile, her eyes staring almost wildly into her mug. She knew nothing about her father, only that he was white. What else could he be, when her mixed-race mother had joked about her being 'quarter-caste'? He had never visited them and had never even been in touch, yet now he was going to force himself into her life, when she was at her most vulnerable?

"I don't know…" Rebecca said hesitantly, but the Social Worker shook her head.

"I'm afraid that it's sorted now, Rebecca. You did say that you were willing to live with whomever your mother suggested."

"She suggested my father? She's not seen him in years!"

"Don't worry, I'm sure you will love getting to know him," the Social Worker said, as though she couldn't care less. "You'll be picked up tomorrow. Do you have all your bits and pieces together?"

"I'll help you pack," Judy said reassuringly, looking up from her hands. Rebecca jumped to her feet and stormed out the room, feeling betrayed by her friends, the Social Worker, the system and, most painfully, her dead mother.

She packed her things silently and realised only when she was sitting down to a quiet dinner with Judy, that she did not even know her father's name. *Gil* seemed to ring a distant bell, but she wasn't sure whether she had just invented the name when she was little, for the sake of other children. She looked across at Judy.

"Sorry," she whispered, "about being so stupid earlier."

"Don't worry about it," Judy laughed quietly, but without even a hint of humour. "You've every right to be nervous and angry, but your mum would've done this for the best."

"What's his name?" she asked, as she squeezed half the bottle of ketchup onto a single chicken nugget.

"Whose?"

"My father's. The person I'm going to live with."

"William," Judy replied, looking down at her own plate of food. "William Gilbert. Your mum didn't talk about him much, but she was really crazy about him." She would not say any more, clearly upset that she had not been given permanent custody, but too controlled or polite to mention it. As they finished their dinner, they talked about school and Rebecca realised she would now have to leave without saying goodbye to her friends. She had only returned to school after her mum's funeral, and she could not explain why or how much she had enjoyed the past two weeks.

After dinner, she went onto *Facebook* and posted a message of farewell to her friends, explaining that she would be leaving the city for the wilds of rural Lincolnshire and had no idea when she would have chance to see them again. Then she flicked through her mum's old posts, to the time before the cancer, and looked to see if William Gilbert was anywhere to be found. There was nothing, just as she had suspected.

Rebecca did not sleep that night, far too nervous about the following day to find any rest in the city that had been her home throughout her life. She listened to the drunks slurring and crashing their way home, the incomprehensible conversations of dealers and pimps, all backed by the familiar sounds of sirens and more expletives than you could fill a dictionary with. It was all she had ever known, and every sound was precious. She had always known that her mum hated it, saying it was no place to bring up a child, but Rebecca had always disagreed, stating her sentimentality as the reason she never wanted to move. A month before her mother had become ill, there had been a knife attack on their street. A young man had been killed and Rebecca's mum had seen it as the right time to look for somewhere else to live. Thoughts of leaving had all stopped along with the diagnosis though.

The night passed too quickly, and Rebecca could not soak in all the sounds and feelings that she wanted to. She got up at about half past six in the morning and, after getting showered and dressed, went through to the Kitchen, confident that she would be the first person in the house to wake up. She had become used to not sleeping during her mum's illness and she had kept a baby monitor by her bed in case her mum had needed her for anything during the night.

She sat for a while, pushing her spoon through the soggy cornflakes but hardly eating any. It was an hour later when Judy got up, brushing sleep out of her eyes and looking irritable and annoyed. Rebecca looked at her and smiled, but neither of them felt like talking so they sat in silence for half an hour before there was a knock on the door.

Rebecca went to answer it, with Judy following behind, a cigarette balanced loosely on her bottom lip. The man who stood there was wearing a scruffy t-shirt and ripped jeans and looked like he enjoyed a couple of pints a night with maybe as many burgers. Rebecca looked at him, uncertain how she should greet her father, who stood silently at the door despite Judy asking him to come in.

"Where's your things, Rebecca?" he asked at last and Rebecca could hardly understand his heavy Lincolnshire accent.

"They're in the Lounge," Judy replied. "I'll bring them through."

The man followed Judy into the room and brought Rebecca's suitcases through before putting them in his car. Then Rebecca put her arms around Judy and said goodbye. It surprised Rebecca that she found it so difficult to say goodbye, despite having lost her mum so recently. Judy had been a constant source of comfort and support, and they both had tears in their eyes as she kissed Rebecca and then led her through to the car.

The car smelt strongly of floral air freshener, which made Rebecca balk. There was a child's seat in the back and suddenly she realised the possibility that she may have younger brothers and sisters.

"Do you have children?" she asked, as the car pulled away and began the long, frustrating drive out of the city.

"Yes," the man replied. "Two."

"So," Rebecca began, trying to start conversation, "what should I call you?"

"Graham," the driver replied, and Rebecca felt her stomach flip as she realised that she had misunderstood the man's identity. Had Judy known that it wouldn't be her father who was coming to collect her, or had she just not cared enough to check?

"Not William Gilbert?" she gasped.

"No," the man said, laughing at the apparent absurdity of the suggestion. "William asked me to come and pick you up, so he could do some last-minute preparations."

Rebecca felt embarrassed but shared in his amusement at the mistaken identity. It made the journey much more comfortable and she enjoyed the rest of it, talking to Graham, who turned out to be funny, friendly and caring, and whose mother had died when he was twelve. He told her candidly about how it had made him feel but explained that he was the eldest of five children, so he'd had to quickly grow up in order to help his father deal with the loss and look after 'the litt'luns'.

They reached Lincolnshire within three hours and Rebecca looked out of her window as Graham explained that this was Seaton, the village where her father lived. Small thatched cottages lined the streets, looking like something out of a television programme and as far removed from Rebecca's home as she could possibly imagine.

"It's not like anywhere I've ever seen," she said softly. "It's like something from *Pride and Prejudice*."

"It's an estate village," Graham said. "That's why it looks like this."

"Estate?" Rebecca repeated. "This is nothing like the estate where I grew up."

Graham laughed. "No, it belongs to the Estate. Well, it used to at any rate. A lot of it was sold off in the '70s."

"Will I be living in one of the thatched houses?" Rebecca asked, but Graham just laughed again and turned off down a small lane which had a sign outside saying 'Private Land'. She looked around her, gazing at what seemed to be miles and miles of woodland and, beyond that, lawns and gardens. It took them five minutes to reach the house, which was three storeys high and wide enough to hold Judy's flat several times over. Graham stopped outside and Rebecca got out, hoping that her father had an upstairs flat in the building as she imagined the view would be spectacular.

A middle-aged man wearing jeans and a yellow shirt, that was dropped casually over his belt, came rushing out and looked at her for a moment before putting his arms around her. Rebecca returned the gesture uneasily and looked at him.

"My God, you really are like your mother. I'm so pleased you're here," he exclaimed. "I'm William Gilbert."

Rebecca did not dare speak in case the man was shocked by her strong accent, as he himself spoke in perfect Queen's English. Graham took Rebecca's bags out of the car and carried them inside the house.

"You must be tired. Travelling always makes one tired," William continued when Rebecca did not say anything. "Come into the house."

"Where do we live?" Rebecca whispered.

"Here," William replied, confusion evident in his voice. "This is Seaton. We don't use the Hall – it was converted into holiday flats years ago. We live in the Lodge."

Rebecca followed her father into the house, feeling more out of place than she ever had done in her life. She could hear her footsteps echo as she stepped over the threshold, and she looked up to see painted portraits lining the walls and an ornate staircase leading to an upper floor, with doors in every direction.

"The Hall is bigger than this?" Rebecca asked as she looked around. "It's a change from Mum's flat."

"I'm so sorry about your mum, Rebecca," William said softly. "She was an incredible person."

"She never mentioned you," Rebecca replied, and then realised how harsh she must have sounded, as her father's face fell. "I mean-"

"Don't worry. We had already separated by the time you were born. Come on into the Living Room." He led her through and waved to Graham as he drove down the long drive and back into the village.

The Living Room was full of antique trinkets and ornaments. Hanging on the wall opposite the door was a large tapestry depicting an Arabian woman dancing, surrounded by men astride camels and, in the background, some strangely disproportionate pyramids. In fact, Rebecca thought as she walked a little further into the room, the entire décor was colonial. Under the tapestry, there was a large fireplace with decorative tiles depicting Indian scenes from the nineteenth century. Rebecca walked over to it and looked at the pictures on the mantelpiece itself. Seven years of her school photographs stared back at her, the most recent one situated in the middle.

"You've got loads of photos of me!" she exclaimed. "How did you get them?"

"Your mum sent me one each year. And she'd always send me a picture of you on your birthday with the Christmas card."

"She never sent you a Christmas card," Rebecca replied, feeling almost afraid of the man behind her. "I know because I used to help her address them all."

As she turned around, William looked at her with a gentle smile which was unbearably patronising. "You know, adults make an appalling habit of keeping secrets from their children. The tea's in the pot, would you like to pour?"

Rebecca looked down at the yellow teapot with confusion. "Does it work the same way as a kettle?" she asked at last. Her father laughed.

"No, you need a tea-strainer." He pointed to a small metal dish on a stick and Rebecca picked it up, utterly baffled.

"Do I put the tea bag in that?" she asked, trying to sound as though she knew what she was doing. Her father just smiled and took the tea-strainer from her.

"Don't worry, I'll do it." He poured the tea straight from the pot, through the strainer, and into beautiful china cups, which were placed on matching saucers. Rebecca looked at her tea and picked up the matching milk jug, pouring as much milk as she could into the small space at the top of the cup. She loathed tea without sugar, but the sugar was in cubes and she wasn't sure whether or not she ought to break them up before using them.

"So," she said, trying to make conversation, "do you look after this for the *National Trust* or something?"

"The Estate? Oh no, my family's – sorry, *our* family's – owned it for years. Around nine hundred and forty actually." He sipped his tea noiselessly, holding the saucer in his left hand as he drank. Rebecca's saucer had been left on the table.

"What, you're like a lord?" she asked after gulping down the last mouthful of tea, only to find that it contained small grains and she had to force it down without gagging.

"No," he replied with a slight laugh. "My father was a baron, but I don't use the title. It's a bit old-fashioned."

Rebecca looked at him, unconvinced. Everything in the house seemed ancient to her and she could not fathom why the man in front of her would live in such a place and yet say that his title was too old-fashioned. She put her cup back on the table, forgetting the saucer, and looked around the room, trying to imagine how her mum could ever have fallen in love with someone who lived like this.

"So, can I go anywhere on the whole Estate?" she asked. It felt strange to use the word 'estate' to mean a large green area, full of trees and gardens and owned by one person. She was mocked at school for being 'from the estate', and that meant something entirely different.

"Well, almost anywhere. The Hall may be locked at this time of year, although there might be birdwatchers in. I can't remember. The tourist board takes care of that. I can always show you around it when there's no one there but I don't like to go in otherwise because I feel it can be somewhat intrusive. Oh, and there's the old Hunting Lodge by the lake. It's a beautiful building but very dangerous so I wouldn't like it if you went in there." There was a pause. "Especially not alone," he added at last, suddenly staring at the large grandfather clock in the corner of the room.

"Dangerous?"

"It's a very old building – Henry the Eighth used it – and the timbers on the roof are rotten.

It's just waiting for a storm to bring it all crashing down. Everywhere apart from that you're welcome to explore."

Rebecca could feel her eyelids becoming heavy, as though the journey had been thousands of miles rather than just three hours in a car. She lifted her hand to her face as she yawned, and William smiled across at her, getting to his feet and putting the cup and saucer gently down on the table.

"Are you tired?"

"A bit," she admitted. There was no point in hiding the fact – the yawn had evidently given her away and she didn't want her father to think she was bored. "I think it's just all so new and different."

"I'll take you up to your room," her father said, as she followed him out and up the stairs. "You can have a rest before we eat."

The stairs were long and spiralling and her room was clearly on the top floor. She wondered how Graham had managed to carry all her things up in one trip. "I would have had it redecorated," William continued, "but in the end the custody hearings concluded quite quickly so I haven't had time." He pushed open the door at the top of the stairs. They were now on the fourth floor of the Lodge as it was an attic room.

"This room always belongs to the eldest child," William said, standing still for a moment to catch his breath. "The view is glorious."

"Was this your room then?" Rebecca asked, looking around at the books and toys that were neatly placed on shelves and in boxes.

"No, it was my brother's." William walked over to the dormer window and opened it up, letting in the warm September breeze.

"I have an uncle?"

"Had. Past tense, I'm afraid. Benjamin died years ago."

"Sorry," she murmured, unsure what else to say.

"Don't worry about it," her father replied. "I picked out some books for you. They're on your bed. I hope they aren't too childish."

Rebecca thanked him, and he nodded.

"I'll call you at dinner time."

He walked out, closing the door behind him and leaving Rebecca in the strange attic room. It was weird to be surrounded by someone else's things, and her own belongings seemed quite meagre compared to them. At any other point in her life, Rebecca would have been curious to investigate every single nook and cranny, but she found she was so tired that her explorer's instinct was lost, and she simply curled up on the bed and fell asleep.

She must have slept the afternoon away and she was certain that she had dreamt about her mum as, when she woke up, she was both distraught and horrified to find that she wasn't in her pokey little room in her mother's council flat. She could hear a strange voice calling her name, then it was suddenly much closer and was accompanied by a knock on her bedroom door.

"Rebecca?" her father called, "are you awake?" She swung her legs around the bed and walked over to the door, opening it to find that William was standing there, now wearing an old Fair Isle jumper over his shirt. "It's become cold," he explained, seeing her looking at his change of clothes. "I'll close the window for you. See you in the Dining Room in a minute." He walked into the room and Rebecca began to wander down the many stairs, realising suddenly that she had no idea which of the numerous doors would lead to a Dining Room. She was not even familiar with having a Dining Room. Everyone she knew ate either in the Living Room or the Kitchen.

William came to her rescue, pointing to the door next to the Living Room, and she walked in. A large table was set in the middle of the room, and there were more portraits hanging on the wall, including one of the man who took the seat opposite her.

"Who are the other people?" she asked him, indicating to the pictures.

"My father," he pointed to the one next to him. "His father, grandfather, et cetera. We'll need to get one of you. You'll inherit this one day and I'm sure your children will want to see you in oils."

They settled down at the neatly laid table and began their meal. Rebecca thought that her father's cooking left a little to be desired but said nothing about it as he was clearly pleased with himself. It looked – and probably tasted – like the sort of thing that TV chefs make, but she found herself wishing for the comforting food that her mum or Judy would make. She poured the tea this time, pleased to demonstrate that she had already learnt something in the short time she had been in the house.

"Do you want to go and sit in the Living Room while I have a cigarette?" her father asked, taking a silver case out of his pocket and opening it to reveal a number of neatly rolled cigarettes. "I know it's a terrible habit but it's a difficult one to break."

"It doesn't bother me. Mum smoked."

"Did she?" William asked, sounding genuinely surprised. He lit the cigarette and leant back to enjoy it. Once he had taken a couple of breaths, he continued talking. "What would you like to do tomorrow?"

"I thought I'd look round the garden," Rebecca replied, closing her eyes and trying to imagine that it was her mum's cigarette smoke that was filling her nostrils.

"Brilliant idea," William replied, stubbing out the cigarette on a glass ashtray with still an inch of it left to smoke. "I'll make a picnic if it's good weather and we can eat it in the orchard."

"Ok." Rebecca stared at the cigarette end, thinking of how much money her mum had spent on cigarettes and wondering what gave the man before her the right to waste so much of them. "Do you have a computer here?"

Her father paused for a moment, looking uncertain. "Yes," he said reluctantly. "It's upstairs in my Study."

"Can I use it then? Please?"

"Alright," he conceded, "but only for half an hour each night."

"Half an hour?"

Facebook and email would provide her with the links she needed to maintain with the world she loved, and half an hour would give Rebecca no time at all to contact everyone.

"I'm sorry, Rebecca," her father said, clearly with no intention of changing his plans, "but I do have to have some rules. The Study is on the first floor and it's the door on the left."

Rebecca got up and left without another word. She was furious that her father could be so unthinking, and angry with her dead mother for thinking that it would be a good idea to leave her in the care of a man whose way of life was so alien to her. William's computer was old and took a long time to load, which made her even angrier as she sat in front of it drumming her fingers on the desk in the way she had seen her mum do.

When at last she had signed in as a guest and logged onto her *Facebook*, she was touched to see many of her friends had posted on her profile. 'Miss you hon' covered the page but the display of affection just made her feel emotional and alone. She typed her status several times, finally posting 'I'm in a weird country house with my dad – a man I only met this morning' and then spent some time chatting with a friend from school who told her that she was missing her in maths and history as she had no one to copy now. Those were the two subjects that Rebecca loved the most, but she had always kept her ability a secret from most of the class as she didn't want to be *that boffin*, preferring to maintain the streetwise label she had acquired simply because of her neighbourhood.

Her half an hour was up before she had done anything, and William came into the room and stood behind her until she turned off the computer and spun around. She was furious with him and could not bring herself even to acknowledge him, choosing instead to storm straight past and up to her bedroom, where she sat for a little while in the window seat, admiring the absolute darkness, something that was totally new to her.

She went to bed early – although she initially struggled to find an upstairs bathroom – and slept easily. The bed was surprisingly comfortable, and the pillow smelt faintly of lavender. She did not dream, but woke up to the sunlight streaming into her room and her father knocking on the door.

"Wake up, Sweetheart," he called. "It's gone ten o'clock. The sun's shining and it's a beautiful day."

She padded over to the door, the bare floorboards feeling strange against her feet, and opened it to smile up at her father. "I was already awake," she lied, and walked past him and down the stairs into the bathroom. He continued talking, which made her feel slightly uncomfortable as she went into the shower, still hearing the comparative stranger speaking to her through the closed door.

"There's cereal out on the breakfast table. I'll get us some lunch sorted and then we can head off. Did you bring any walking boots?"

"No," she called back, trying to stop herself from sarcastically asking why a city girl would have walking boots. "Why? Do I need them?"

"I'll see if there are any in the cupboard."

William's cupboard was clearly full of many things and, once she had showered and eaten her breakfast, Rebecca found a pair of ladies' walking boots waiting beside the door. They were a size too big – her mum's size, in fact – but there was an unopened pair of insoles sticking out of one of them. She pulled them on and went outside to where her father was standing looking out at the grounds, as though he was seeing them for the first time.

They walked for the remainder of the morning without saying much, but Rebecca found the silent company surprisingly enjoyable. The gardens were enormous, and stretched a long way in each direction, so that the house was surrounded by vast green spaces. William explained that the Lodge was at the end of a mile of drive, but the Hall itself – which she only saw from a distance – was in the middle of the grounds, with three miles of garden and land in each direction.

"There are farms too," her father said as they walked through the cultivated gardens, which were still full of beautiful blooms. "Well, one farm now. There were three when I was younger, but my father sold two of them off. I try not to bother the farmer but I'm sure he wouldn't mind if we arranged a visit at some point."

Rebecca just smiled across and said nothing. She had visited a farm once as part of an initiative to educate city children about the countryside, and she had not enjoyed it much. She was not bothered in any way by animals, neither frightened of them nor enchanted by them, and the farm had been a tedious experience.

There were walled gardens as well, and William led her through them all. One of them, he explained, was used by the local primary-school children to grow vegetables, and the harvest was imminent. Rebecca was more excited about this, and made her father promise that she could work with the children when they came. She loved little kids, and one of the only regrets she had ever had about being from a single parent family was that there had been no prospect of younger brothers and sisters. Her mum had never had a relationship for as long as she could remember.

For the most part, William and Rebecca walked through the open land in silence and enjoyed the early autumn sunshine and the smells, sights and sounds of the countryside. William had clearly always loved this, and Rebecca found it weirdly attractive. Rebecca was actually disappointed when her father started to make conversation again, shattering the enjoyable silence.

"I don't think your mother ever felt comfortable in this place," he muttered softly, looking around.

"Why not?"

"She found it a little overbearing," William explained. "It can't have helped that my father was still alive then. He struggled a lot with illness for decades and he was reaching the end of his life. He would get very angry."

"Because you were so much older than Mum?" Rebecca asked, although she privately wondered if it had more to do with the colour of her mother's skin.

"Possibly," her father replied. "Maybe also because I hadn't turned out to be the person he wanted. And a couple of other things that seemed important at the time." There was a tone of sad resignation in William's voice and the twelve-year-old girl could tell that he was regretting something.

"Did you and mum get engaged?"

Now he sounded genuinely surprised, even hurt. "Engaged? Rebecca, we were married for five years. She never mentioned any of this to you?"

"No, sorry," Rebecca replied, feeling guilty. "She used to joke about my dad being a sailor in the Navy."

"Well she told you one true thing about me then," her father said with a slight laugh. "I was a Lieutenant in the Royal Navy during the Falklands. That's how your mother and I met. Her father and I had served together so I went to his funeral."

Rebecca paused. She knew almost as little about her grandparents as she did about her father, but William's words were not a revelation. She must have just forgotten that her grandfather had been in the Navy.

"She used to call me *Gil*," her father continued. "I was introduced to her by another old colleague as Gilbert, rather than William."

"Did you like the Navy?" Rebecca asked.

"Not particularly. I joined to please my father."

"But I guess it didn't work?" Rebecca said, running her hand absent-mindedly along the top of the long grasses that grew beside the path. William answered, but she did not hear his words as her hand suddenly brushed against nothing and she looked to see an overgrown path leading further into the grounds.

"Where does that go?" she asked, pointing.

"It's not a path," her father replied. "Please don't go down there, Rebecca." Despite having only known him for a day, Rebecca could tell from his tone that she shouldn't push the subject any further, but her curiosity was getting the better of her.

"But where does it go?" she persisted, straining her eyes to see if she could work out where the path would take her.

"Nowhere," her father said abruptly, taking her sleeve and pulling her away. "Come on, there are plenty of beautiful places you *can* go."

They shared lunch in the orchard, which was old and beginning to bear less and less fruit. William explained his plans for planting new trees and suggested that, at some point, they could go to the garden centre and choose them together. Rebecca smiled and nodded but could not seem to explain to the man before her that she had no knowledge of trees, having grown up in the city to love and rely on grey concrete as a sign of home.

They spent the rest of the day in the grounds but when the evening came and found them both outside, it brought a warning chill which made them hurry back to the Lodge together, laughing. But no matter what was discussed, Rebecca could not stop thinking about her father's reaction to the path she had found earlier that morning. She had put her suspicions to the test by enquiring about another overgrown path, only to find her father had been interested in finding out where that would lead.

"I had a great time today, Rebecca," William said as he removed his hat and scarf and placed them over the large wax coat on the tall coat-stand.

"It was really fun." Rebecca paused. "Thanks."

"You can call me 'Dad', you know," William called as he walked through to the Kitchen and washed his hands before opening the cupboard to ponder the possibilities for dinner.

"No, I don't think I can," Rebecca mumbled, following him into the Kitchen. "I'm really sorry."

"Well," William said, pulling a packet of fusilli out of the cupboard and looking at it thoughtfully, "I certainly don't want you to feel pressurised into anything. Do you want to watch TV while I make dinner?"

"I think I'll just go upstairs," she replied, and wandered up the many stairs to her room before sitting down on the bed and looking nervously out of the window. She wondered if she could see the path from her room but, in the dusk, it was difficult to make out anything, and she was sure that the path was further into the grounds. She moved onto the cold window-seat and pressed her face against the glass, but saw nothing that gave away the location of the mysterious path.

She pulled away from the window and sat down on the bed, looking around her at the toys and books that had remained untouched for so long. There were toy-boxes painted in a variety of shades and she discovered that they contained a number of toy soldiers and model farm animals. Although they did not interest her, she had also seen a beautiful teddy bear, which she could not help but admire, despite the fact that she had given away all her soft toys four years ago.

This bear was sitting looking at her from the top of one of the toy-boxes, its head slightly tilted so that, with the light shining in its glass eyes, it had a strange expression on its face. It was unclothed apart from a blue ribbon around its neck and a metal button in its left ear, with a tattered label. Rebecca picked it up and held it to her face. It smelt old and musty, and she wondered how long it had been sitting here alone.

After she realised how childish she looked, she placed it lovingly on the bedside table and picked up one of the books, an old hardback called The KNIGHTS of THE ROUND TABLE by the wonderfully-named Moira F. Doolan. Rebecca knew the Arthurian legends, but she looked through the book and found that she did not know many of these. It was an old book, from the 1950s and, like the teddy bear, she wondered how many years had passed since it had been used, or even held. It made her think about the uncle that she had only just learnt about, and she wondered when he had died and what had happened to him. She found herself morbidly considering whether his death had been sudden or whether it had happened over a prolonged and painful period of time, as it had for her mother. The thoughts made her cry, something that felt very strange to her and, picking up her pillow as though it was a soft toy, she sobbed into it. The lavender filled her nostrils and reminded her of a scent from a long time ago which, although she could not identify the memories attached to it, just made her cry even more.

"I miss you, Mum," she cried, feeling the pillow gradually dampen with her tears. "I'm scared of this place. I'm scared by not knowing what's down that path." She threw the pillow down on the bed and buried her head in it, letting the pent-up tears fall until she felt better for her emotional outburst.

William was none the wiser about her tears at dinner and the conversation was light and easy, mostly about the weather which, her father assured her, was typical for a Lincolnshire autumn. Rebecca was getting better at using the saucers, but she knew that she held her knife and fork in the wrong way, much to her father's amusement and her annoyance. She had never had much patience with the idea of the upper-classes, and here she found herself as one of them and struggling to fit in. When at last it was time for bed, she was grateful to get away from facing the massive changes to her life and talking to the father she hardly knew and had nothing in common with.

She set an early alarm, determined to be up with the sunlight to discover where the overgrown path would take her. Her mum had always said 'the only thing we have to fear is fear itself', and Rebecca's understanding of that philosophy was that seeing where the path led would allow her to lose that fear of the unknown.

Despite her determination to uncover the secret, she was not impressed when her alarm woke her early the following morning. For a while, she lay in bed deliberating whether or not she should leave the comfort of her room, but curiosity got the better of her. She dressed quickly and quietly and, for the first morning in as long as she could remember, she did not take a shower. Pulling on her borrowed walking boots, she crept out of the house and into the gardens, which were gleaming in the early autumn morning.

She found the path easily enough, following the recently trampled grass that they had walked along yesterday. When she reached the turn-off, Rebecca once again pondered the sense in what she was doing. She hoped that the path would not get her lost in the vast gardens of the Estate as she did not know what her strange father would be like when angry. Once again, though, she felt the pull of curiosity and began to walk along the path, admiring the sparkle of the grass in the early morning dew.

The path came to an abrupt stop in front of a picturesque lake. There were bulrushes all around it and several mallards were paddling their way across the water, the sun shining on the drakes' magnificent colours and making the females seem elegant beyond anything Rebecca had ever imagined possible for ducks. She had always thought they were the watery equivalent of pigeons.

There was a small pier in the lake and an old rowing boat was moored to it, bobbing up and down with the gentle movement of the wind on the water. At the other side of the lake, a good five minutes' walk away, was the old Hunting Lodge which her father had warned her about on her arrival two days ago. She could see from where she stood that it was in a state of disrepair and she did not wish to put herself in danger by going too close to it.

It was all beautiful and peaceful beyond words, and Rebecca stood for a while trying to soak it all in, imagining beautiful summer days here and wondering whether the lake froze over in the winter, like lakes in films she had seen. She imagined herself skating on the ice but then it dawned on her that she had no idea how deep and dangerous the water was. She bent down, picked up a small rock and threw it into what looked to be the deepest point of the lake, being careful not to catch any of the ducks, although they noticed the disturbance and frantically splashed their way out of the water.

"All along the back water."

Rebecca jumped. In the stillness, it sounded as though the voice had come from directly behind her.

"Mr Gilbert?" she called, trying to steady her voice, although she was sure her nervousness was evident in her tone. She was equally certain that the voice did not belong to her father.

"Through the rushes tall."

Now the sound seemed to be coming from within the bulrushes. They were too dense and tall to see if anyone was indeed hiding in them, but Rebecca thought she would have seen movement if there was anyone there.

"Hello?" she said, beginning to walk backwards along the path, fast enough to get away but slow enough to make it appear that she was not scared.

"Ducks-are-a-dabbling," gabbled the voice, now obviously a child. "Up tails all!"

Rebecca suddenly became terrified and, turning on her heel, she ran as swiftly as her walking boots would allow. She could feel the spongey ground sinking slightly beneath her feet, but her determination and fear spurred her on. At last, she was on the more familiar path back to the house, where she continued to run until she literally bumped into her father.

"Rebecca!" he gasped, looking at her in surprise. "Calm down! What on earth is the matter?"

Rebecca could not think of how to approach the subject so took a moment to catch her breath. "Does anyone else live on the Estate?"

"No," William replied. "I checked. There's no one in the Hall at the moment and, other than that, it's only you and me. The cleaning lady, Matilda, comes every morning though. Oh, and Graham does some bits and bobs in the garden, but he's gone down to London today."

"No one apart from them?" Rebecca asked.

"No. Well, it gets used for dog-walking sometimes, but-"

"By children?"

"Sometimes, I suppose," William shrugged. "Why, did you see someone?"

"No," Rebecca said, calming down as they began walking back to the house together. "I thought I heard someone, that's all."

"It's a very still day," her father said as they walked. "A voice could have carried a long way in any direction." Rebecca agreed, thankful that her father was thinking so practically about the matter, and wondering what had caused her judgement to slip.

"What were you doing out so early?" he asked after a moment.

"I wanted to see where that path would lead," Rebecca replied honestly, hoping her bluntness would make her father less angry.

"You went down to the lake?" William stopped dead in his tracks, not angry but clearly horrified. "What did this voice sound like?"

"Like a little boy laughing at me," Rebecca said, trying to calm her heartbeat, which was pounding at the sudden change in her father's behaviour and attitude. "I think he was saying a poem."

"You shouldn't have gone down to the lake, Rebecca," her father said firmly. "I told you; it's really dangerous."

"No," she argued, annoyed by how much he was frightening her, "you said that the Hunting Lodge was dangerous. And I didn't go in there."

William continued walking but made it very clear that his daughter should follow and listen to him as he went. "Rebecca, I'm going out later today. I was going to say that you could stay here on your own, but I don't want you going down to the lake." He paused. "Especially when I'm not here."

Rebecca nodded slowly. "Where are you going?"

"The Estate Agents in town. I'm thinking about putting some of the cottages up for let. Bring in some money for your school fees."

"School fees?"

"Yes," William replied, a note of confusion in his voice as clear as the disdain in Rebecca's own. "What's wrong with that?"

"Nothing," she muttered, "but I've never had a problem with normal schools."

Her father suddenly looked very harassed, scratching his chin with his thumb.

"Can we talk about this another time? Look, can I trust you to stay in the house or will you have to come into town with me?"

"I promise I'll stay in the house," she said softly. "Can I use the internet while you're out?"

"Of course," William replied, sounding relieved, and Rebecca was grateful that her father was relaxing his rule about the amount of time she could spend on the computer.

He left after lunch, telling her to keep the door locked and not to light any candles, backing up his concerns with a brief lecture on the dangers of leaving candles unattended in any house, let alone one with long curtains and old carpets. Beyond those two rules, she was allowed to do anything she liked during his absence.

She waved him off as he drove away, before turning back to the house and wondering what she could do to make the most of having the place to herself. Although she couldn't have explained why, she did not want to go on the computer and finally she decided to investigate her father's Study. William had not forbidden her, so she worked her way through twelve ledgers and handfuls of photographs and bank statements before finding a black edged photo album which, upon opening, she found to be full of yellowed newspaper cuttings. The first one was from July 1968 and had as its headline 'Tragedy Strikes at Seaton Manor'. Curious, and slightly afraid, Rebecca read through the article.

Tragedy struck at the heart of Seaton yesterday as local heir, Benjamin Gilbert, drowned in a boating accident. Benjamin, known as Benjy, died after falling into the lake on the family Estate. When his parents could not find the boy, a search was launched, leading to the discovery of the ten-year-old's body.

Benjamin had been boating on the lake with his younger brother, William. A friend of the family said the boys were close and enjoyed outdoor pursuits together, such as boating, fishing and shooting.

Rebecca turned the page, not believing what was in front of her, but determined to find out as much as she could about whatever had happened. She found the next article to be called 'Baron's Son Buried in Local Churchyard' and she read on with morbid interest and fascination.

Local heir, Benjamin Gilbert, was laid to rest in St Peter's church in a small and intimate service on Friday morning. The victim of a tragic boating accident, Benjamin was the eldest son of Baron Francis and Lady Margaret Gilbert, and the only brother of William.

In a touching tribute, William read his brother's favourite poem at the graveside and could be seen weeping with his mother and father.

The family have thanked all those on the Estate and beyond for their support during the last week, saying that it has been the one thing that has kept them going throughout the ordeal.

Rebecca put the book down, not wanting to read on any further. She did not want to know which poem her father had read at his brother's graveside and neither did she want to go upstairs. She was horrified at the idea of resting on the bed that had belonged to the young boy who had met a watery death near the place she had so passionately admired that morning.

She was quiet that evening and told her father she was feeling sick. He was worried and disappointed but led her upstairs and closed the open window.

"I'll leave the door open in case you need me," he said, pulling it to, without latching it shut. He walked downstairs, and Rebecca tried to get to sleep. She could hear her father's television programme and enjoyed the background noise for a while before she finally drifted off.

In her dreams she was running through the Estate until she reached the path leading down to the lake. It was slightly more overgrown than she remembered, but a strange feeling of curiosity pulled her along, almost against her will.

"All along the back water," whispered the same voice that she had heard earlier in the day, "through the rushes tall."

She had reached the lake to find it looking as beautiful as it had done before, sparkling in the sunlight, crowned in tall bulrushes with ducks swimming peacefully across the surface. The boat, however, was missing and in its place was a pool of deep, black water.

"Mum?" she called, suddenly afraid. "Mum!" Her mother did not hear or answer her, but the black water began to swirl around, like whirlpools she had seen in apocalyptic films, and a child's hand began to rise out of the water. She could hear someone in the distance calling her name, a voice she seemed to recognise but could not place who it was. Light flooded into her room as the curtains opened and she sat up, wide awake.

Her father stood over her, a look of puzzled concern on his face. "Are you alright, Rebecca, Sweetheart?" he asked, sitting on the edge of her bed and squeezing her feet gently and reassuringly through the covers. "You were screaming."

"I just had a nightmare," Rebecca replied, wiping her eyes with her hand and smiling at her father's attempt to make her feel better.

"Anything you'd like to talk about?" William asked, turning slightly to face her, although he seemed anything but comfortable.

"Not really," Rebecca sighed. "It was about ducks."

"Ducks?"

"Yeah." A pause followed, in which the room fell into a strange silence. "It's stupid. Sorry I woke you up."

"You didn't," her father replied slowly. "I was just going to make a cup of coffee and take it into the garden. It's another beautiful day." He gestured out of the window to where the Estate lay, basking in glorious autumn sunshine.

"To the lake?"

"No," said her father, giving her a puzzled look. "I'll go back to the orchard. It's my favourite spot. Would you like to join me?"

"No thanks," Rebecca replied, realising that it had been two days since she had showered, and her room had become very warm during the night. "I'll just have something downstairs."

"You know," William said gently, standing up and looking out of the window. Once again, it seemed as though he had forgotten how beautiful his home was until seeing through his daughter's eyes. "Your nightmare wasn't real. You're quite safe here."

"Thanks," Rebecca smiled. "I'm sure I'll get used to it. Can I take a picnic lunch into the garden again?"

"Of course," her father replied, beaming at the suggestion. "Would you like me to come with you? I don't mind either way. I can certainly keep myself busy with some paperwork but it's nothing that can't go on hold until tomorrow."

"No, it's alright. I won't go to the Hall or the Hunting Lodge, so I'll be fine."

Rebecca had positioned her promise to her father very carefully and, although he was satisfied, she was pleased that he had not demanded that she stay away from the lake.

As soon as she had showered and eaten her breakfast, she left the house, forgetting that her father had promised to give her a picnic. She walked briskly down the path to the lake and stood for a while near the pier, trying to come to terms with the idea that something so terrible could ever have happened in such a beautiful spot. The ducks moved noiselessly across the water, as they had done in her dream, but the surface was otherwise very peaceful.

"I wonder if there's another lake on the Estate," she mused, trying to reconcile herself with the idea, when she heard rustling in the grasses behind her.

"Ducks are a-dabbling," said the child's voice, slightly more determined this time, as though he was daring Rebecca, in a friendly way, to stay.

"What do you want?" she demanded, still not turning around.

"Don't you like my poem?"

"It isn't your poem," she replied, to a disappointed silence. "I've heard it before somewhere."

"Try and find it then," the boy said. "You won't."

Rebecca laughed at the challenge. "There are thousands of books in the house. It's got to be in one of them."

"I'll bet it isn't," the child retorted. "I'll bet that you can't find it in a single one!" He sounded friendly and playful, and it suddenly occurred to Rebecca that he may not be a ghost at all.

"If I turn around, will I see you?" she asked slowly.

"Of course," the boy replied, openly laughing at her. She turned around. She saw no ghost, only a boy a couple of years younger than her, staring at her with laughing eyes and unable to contain his amusement. He was wearing a stripy t-shirt with light coloured trousers and had very blond hair. She suddenly felt ridiculous.

"You don't look like a-" she stopped, wondering how to explain to the boy in front of her that she had mistaken him for a ghost.

"Like a what?"

"Like a ghost. You don't look like a ghost."

The boy smiled. "But I must sound like one," he replied. "Last time I tried to start a conversation with you, you ran away."

"Sorry," Rebecca muttered, hating the word. She was unsure how to talk to the boy in front of her, who was unashamedly trespassing on the Estate. "Why are you here? This is private land, you know."

"I like the ducks," said the boy, as though it was the most obvious thing in the world and excused his trespassing. "I've always liked the ducks."

The sun shone down on the two of them and, when Rebecca took a step closer to the water, she noticed with a start that hers was the only shadow. The boy in front of her was solid and lifelike, but the sun shone straight through him as though he was nothing more than a pillar of smoke in the still day. She looked at him with horror and he smiled back reassuringly.

"You *are* a ghost," she murmured. His smile just became wider and they both began to laugh. Their amusement was cut short, however, when they heard the sound of someone running along the path and Rebecca's father calling out her name.

"We've been rumbled!" the boy exclaimed dramatically. "See you tomorrow?"

"Yes, yes, of course." The boy hurried into the bulrushes, which moved for a moment and then became completely still.

"Are you still there?" Rebecca hissed, but there was no reply apart from the jovial quacking of the ducks as they propelled themselves across the clear water.

"Oh, Rebecca!" her father gasped as he burst into sight and saw her. He was out of breath from running and was clutching a full paper bag in his hand. "Here you are! What are you doing here? You promised you would stay away from this place."

"I still haven't been in the Hunting Lodge," Rebecca replied, looking across to where the dilapidated building hulked over the lake. "I came here because..." her voice trailed off as she wondered how to approach the subject with the man in front of her, who seemed so much harder to talk to than the ghost she had just met. "Well, I found an old newspaper cutting yesterday. While you were at the Estate Agent's."

"About what happened?" her father guessed correctly. Rebecca stood still and bowed her head, wishing that he would get cross with her.

"Yes," she whispered. "To your brother. Were you here?"

"Yes."

"What happened?"

"I won't talk about it here, Rebecca," William said firmly, looking around at the lake with suspicion, as though he expected to see the ghost himself. "I don't feel at all comfortable in this place."

They walked back to the house in silence and went straight into the Living Room. William gave his daughter a glass of juice before moving over to the crystal decanter and pouring himself a large glass of whisky. They sat down for a while and William rested his head against his hand, looking old and worried, and Rebecca felt slightly guilty for bringing her father such troubles after only being in his house for a couple of days. It did nothing, however, to quell her curiosity regarding what she had seen about the events at the lake.

"Please," she said after a while, "tell me about Benjamin."

Her father took a deep breath and looked hard at her, as though he did not want to answer the question until he knew her better. Perhaps that was why his answer, when it came, was cautious and hesitant. "He was three years older than me. My parents were both very fair to us, but he was the heir and I was not allowed to forget it."

"But what was he like?"

"He was," William paused, a pained smile on his face for a moment before he regained his composure and looked straight at the girl in front of him. "He was cheeky, fun... I looked up to him a lot. My father took all his investments very seriously and was often away in London for long periods of time to see how they were coming along. So, Benjy was the man I aspired to be. Even when he was only six."

"He was ten when he died, wasn't he?"

"Yes. It was my seventh birthday. My father was home for the weekend and Benjy offered to take me out on the boat."

"And he fell out?"

"Yes. He was... playing. He fell backwards and hit his head on the boat. He sank almost immediately." There was a silence in the room and, although Rebecca opened her mouth to speak, no sound came out as she imagined the situation with grim horror. "I tried to catch hold of him," her father continued slowly, as though he was thinking of things that he had not spoken about in his entire life, "but I couldn't. By the time my parents heard me screaming, he couldn't be found. His body had become entangled in the bulrushes."

"That's awful," Rebecca whispered, still hardly able to find her voice. The loss of her mum had been bad enough, but she had been prepared for that at least, and had appreciated the opportunity to start accepting the situation alongside her mother.

"Yes," William said. "Yes, it was awful. My parents had the bulrushes removed and all the ducks shot. My mother even wanted to drain the lake and fill it in, but my father refused."

"There are lots of rushes there now," Rebecca said softly, walking over to the decanter and pouring her father another glass of whisky. He thanked her before taking a long sip.

"Yes, I planted them just after my father died. The lake always seemed very naked without them." He finished the whisky in one long gulp and then took a deep breath. "There. That's everything you could possibly wish to know about Benjamin. Is there anything else, Sweetheart?"

"Just one more thing," Rebecca said hesitantly. "Do you know a poem that starts 'all along the back water'?"

"Yes, of course," William said, with an uneasy smile. "You mean *Duck's Ditty*, don't you? 'All along the back water, through the rushes tall, ducks are a-dabbling, up tails all'."

"That's it. Who wrote it?"

"Kenneth Grahame. It's in *The Wind in the Willows*."

"That's one of the books in my bedroom!" Rebecca said with realisation. "One of the ones you left out. But there are pages missing from it."

"Oh yes, I'd forgotten," William said. "I tore them out when I was younger. I'm afraid I tried to get rid of anything that made me think of him."

"I understand," Rebecca said sagely. "I thought about getting rid of some of Mum's things but, in the end, Judy took them."

"I'm so sorry about your mum, Rebecca," William whispered into his whisky glass. "We had a great relationship for a while."

"What happened?"

"Look, Rebecca, I will tell you about it, but I'm shattered right now."

"Sorry."

"Don't be," her father said firmly. "I just usually avoid thinking of Benjamin. When I do it brings up all sorts of terrible memories." Rebecca nodded and began walking away, but William took hold of her arm, gently but firmly. "Don't go down to the lake again, Rebecca. It's dangerous." He let his grip slide and got out of his chair as his daughter left the room.

Rebecca felt at once annoyed and sympathetic. Her father had clearly been traumatised by his brother's death and she could understand that. During her mother's illness, there had been a week when her mum had gone into a hospice so that Rebecca could go to a camp with other children whose parents were terminally ill or had just died. It had sounded like a silly, macabre idea but Rebecca had found it therapeutic to share her fears and sadness with other young people who genuinely understood them. Some of the children there were bitter, others terrified, others angry and then there were the children who could not talk about it, many of whom had been sent to the camp, like Rebecca, by their dying parent. William, she realised, was one who kept it all to himself.

She did not pay his concerns any attention, however, and the following day found her at the lakeside once again, sitting on the edge of the pier with her bare feet splashing in the water. The ducks were swimming around her, and she found herself wondering whether any of them were descendants of the birds who had been shot simply for being alive at the time that another life had ended.

"Hello?" she called after a time. "Did you come?" She felt silly calling out for a ghost but sure enough, the bulrushes rustled and the young boy came out, his hair tousled with long grasses. It would never have occurred to Rebecca that he had come from anywhere more ethereal than the waving bulrushes.

"Yes," he said simply, brushing down his clothes.

"What's your name?"

"Benjy. Did you find my poem?"

"No," Rebecca conceded. "It had been torn out of all the books. I've got your copy of *The Wind in the Willows,* but the pages are missing."

"I told you so," Benjy said with a triumphant laugh. "It won't be anywhere in the whole house."

"You're younger than me, aren't you?" Rebecca asked, but it was hardly a question as she already knew the answer.

"Not really," the ghost replied. "I have seen many more years than you."

Rebecca looked around her. Grey clouds were beginning to form in the sky and she became afraid that poor weather would stop her coming down to the lake. "Are you always here?" she asked. "I mean, do you stay at the lake all the time?"

"Time for me is different from how it is for you," Benjy explained. "But yes, I stay around the lake and watch the ducks."

"Do you ever see my father?" Rebecca asked, picking at the pier and throwing the shards of wood into the water, where they floated along the top. "He's your brother, isn't he?"

"Will? No, I never see him. Well, apart from yesterday, that is. He grew up and tried to forget me."

"He found it difficult to think about you," Rebecca said defensively. "He was only seven when..."

"Of course," Benjamin said, clearly irritated. "He stayed in the boat and watched me drown."

"Don't say that," Rebecca chided, although she was unsure why she was defending the father who would tell her so little and whose enigmatic nature was both terrifying and patronising. "He seems really upset about it all."

"Oh, my apologies!" Benjy exclaimed, jumping to his feet and looking very annoyed. "I suppose that he didn't tell you everything that happened that day?"

"His seventh birthday."

"Yes," the ghost replied, his arms crossed and a matter-of-fact tone in his voice. "I bought him a pair of gold cufflinks that came all the way from London."

"Cufflinks?"

"It was a different time then," Benjy said with a carefree wave of his hand. "I thought Will would love them, but he was... careless enough to drop them in the lake. I tried to retrieve them but I... fell into the water."

"Yes," Rebecca said sympathetically, as though it was quite an ordinary conversation. "And you hit your head on the side of the boat?"

"That's not what happened!" the boy said, confusion replacing his look of disgust. "I was awake all the time. I felt myself sinking and tried to swim. But I got caught in the rushes."

"You must have been terrified," Rebecca said gently, laying her hand on the boy's own. It felt warm and not at all how she would have imagined a ghost.

"No. No, I wasn't. It seems strange to say but I was certain that someone would come and drag me out."

"But they didn't come quick enough?"

"Quick enough?" Benjamin laughed. "How could they even know? By the time William started calling out, I was already trapped. And you can't scream when you're at the bottom of a lake." A short silence followed his words and the ducks quacked merrily, not intimidated in the slightest by the two children, who were separated from one another by death alone.

"It must have been really hard for your parents," Rebecca said at last, as the wind picked up and the water suddenly became cold. She took her feet out of the water and let Benjamin dry them on his shirt.

"I never saw my mother again," he sighed. "She died a short while after. My father used to come down here when he was an old man."

"Did you talk to him?"

"He didn't seem to hear me. I always made sure that I recited the poem for him though, just in case."

"Why that particular poem?"

The ghost shrugged as the first few spots of rain began to fall on them. "'Ducks are a-dabbling'. I always loved the ducks here."

With the onset of the first rain that Rebecca had experienced since she arrived, Benjamin left her. He explained that, despite being dead, he was still not keen on the poor weather.

She walked slowly back to the house, wondering whether her mother had ever seen Benjy and, if she had, whether she had ever told William. She missed her mum more every time she thought about her, and had not realised that her father had clearly lost his mother at a young age too. As she walked through the rain, she wondered why William had not called for help sooner. Had he wanted his older brother to drown?

When she arrived back at the Lodge, she went straight to her room, where her father had left her a plate of food and a note on personalised paper. She picked it up and looked at William's scrawled handwriting, which was hardly legible.

Gone down to Boat House to meet with Victor Mallory (Estate Agent). Tried to find you for lunch but couldn't look everywhere! Hope you like cheese sandwiches. William/Dad

She took a bite into the cheese sandwich and discovered that she liked it very much. It wasn't like the cheese she was used to, but she had to admit to herself that it was impressive, and she enjoyed it. There was a packet of salt and vinegar crisps too and a bottle of juice which she polished off quickly, surprisingly hungry after being out in the rain.

After she had eaten, she changed into her pyjamas and picked up Benjy's copy of *The Wind in the Willows*. It was well-read, and the pages were yellow-brown with age. There were illustrations by E. H. Shepherd on the back of the book, depicting Toad gradually falling out of a boat. It made her shudder to think her uncle had met his end in that way. Trying to get rid of those thoughts, she skimmed through the book to make sure that the poem was not there. She couldn't get into the story itself, as she was too old for stories about talking animals. *Duck's Ditty* was quite definitely absent from the book, and she wondered if William regretted tearing the pages out. She was certainly pleased to know that Judy had her mum's things, rather than them lying in a skip somewhere.

She walked around the house for a while, finding the only locked door to be her father's bedroom, and eventually wandered into the Living Room, put the television on and watched old American detective dramas. She was halfway through *Murder, She Wrote* when she heard the front door open and her father calling her name.

"Hello," he said, poking his head around the door. "I bought fish and chips for dinner. Do you like them?"

"Thanks." Rebecca beamed at the thought of having some normal food, but she knew she had certain things she needed to discuss with her father. She took her opportunity as they sat down together at the Dining Room table, eating fish and chips with their fingers and drinking cola out of champagne flutes, which had been Rebecca's suggestion.

"What are cufflinks?" she asked, licking her fingers after the last chip and appreciating the salt and vinegar taste.

"They're what you use instead of buttons on shirt cuffs," her father replied, pushing away the remainder of his fish and chips and leaning back on his chair. "Men's shirts used to have two holes on the cuff, instead of one and a button. People don't really use them much now, apart from at weddings and such, but when I was little my father would never leave the house without them." He took a sip from his glass. "Why do you ask?"

"Do you have a pair?"

"I have several," William said with a smile. "All of my father's and a number of my own."

"What were your first pair like?" Rebecca asked, and her father's face fell as he began to realise where the conversation was heading.

"Erm, well, let's see. My mother bought me a pair for Christmas when I was seven. They were gold, with my initials engraved on. No mean feat considering I have four names!" He paused and looked hard at his daughter. "You're asking some strange questions."

"Sorry," Rebecca muttered, but with no intention of stopping the interrogation. "So, you never had a pair before that?" She knew she had pushed things too far when her father sat up straight in his chair and stared directly into her eyes, visibly annoyed. Much the same look that she had seen his brother give earlier on during the day.

"What did you find, Rebecca?" he demanded.

"Nothing."

"I won't be angry. I just want to know if you've been in my Study again."

"No," Rebecca said, now equally annoyed. "It was just something I saw on TV."

"About my first pair of cufflinks?" William said sarcastically. He looked at his daughter and shook his head. When he spoke again his tone was much gentler. "I did have another pair, but I lost them shortly after I received them." He began tidying up the table, and Rebecca helped him but could not allow herself to stop questioning.

"Where did you get them from?"

William shook his head. "I hope you won't mind if I tell you that this conversation is making me nervous. You couldn't spare me from a couple of these questions, could you?" He dropped the packaging straight into the tall bin outside and then walked back into the house, looking thoughtfully up at the portrait of his father. For the first time, Rebecca noticed that the gap between her father's and her grandfather's portraits was rather large. Perhaps, she thought, that was Benjy's space.

"Sorry," Rebecca said again, this time with more conviction. She felt guilty for upsetting her father, although she was becoming increasingly concerned by his determination to keep secrets. "Do you mind if I go out again?"

"Yes, actually I do," William replied, and Rebecca was too surprised to be indignant. "It's getting dark outside and you don't know the Estate well enough to be able to remember where you can and can't go." He looked down from the portrait and smiled across at her; a warm, nervous smile that tempered Rebecca's anger at his avoidance of the topics she wanted to discuss. They walked through to the Living Room and sat down on different sofas.

"Do you mind if I ask another question then?" Rebecca said. "Since I'm not allowed to go out."

"Fire away," William said, walking over to the decanter and pouring himself a large glass of whisky, from which he took a sip as he slowly walked back to his seat.

"Why did you replant the bulrushes if you never go down to the lake?"

William rolled his eyes at the continuous questioning about the lake but was evidently relieved by the practicality of the question. "I thought it was wrong without it. I used to go down there occasionally." He paused and looked at her, "I'm sure I've already told you this."

"Not really."

"Well, anyway, the local community wanted the lake returned to its natural state."

"Why?"

"Well," William said, shuffling around on the sofa, "the Estate hasn't changed much over the years. My parents' attack on the lake meant that a lot of the natural habitat was lost. I could correct some of the mistakes, so I did."

"When did the ducks come back?"

"There was never really a long time without them," William said thoughtfully, clearly casting his mind back over the years. "My mother hated them."

"She died just after Benjamin," Rebecca muttered.

"Yes, she did. Poor woman, I can't imagine her feeling of loss. The local paper printed an obituary which claimed she died of a broken heart." William took a long drink from the glass until there was little more than a drop left.

"What is that?" Rebecca asked, indicating to the whisky.

William looked confused for a moment but then gave a broad smile. "Twenty-one-year-old *Old Pulteney*," he said. "Arguably the best whisky in the world."

"Mum liked whisky," Rebecca whispered, "but she would never have been able to afford the best stuff in the world."

"Your mum liked whisky?"

"Yes. She said it made her think of happier times."

"She never used to like it," William said, his eyes sparkling slightly. "She used to drink it with me because my father said that no lady would drink scotch. They hated each other."

"Why?"

"My father was a very old-fashioned man, Rebecca," William said gently, "and he could not reconcile himself with having a daughter-in-law who had a different colour skin to him." Rebecca smiled, pleased that her father was being honest with her, and leant across and put her hand gently on his arm. He sat very still, hardly breathing.

"What happened between you?"

"She had an accident on the Estate while she was pregnant," William muttered, "and she realised that this wasn't a safe place to start a family. We talked about moving away, but my father forbade it. I was the surviving heir to Seaton and he wanted it to stay in the family. The only option he gave us was to divorce."

"And she dropped everything. Even your name."

"No," her father said with a smile. "She kept my name. That's why your name is Williams. Her maiden name was Porter." Rebecca's eyes widened at the revelation and her father chuckled into his empty glass, looking at her warmly.

Rebecca did not talk much after yet another revelation about her personal history, and they spent the rest of the evening watching television. There was nothing very interesting on, and her father soon fell asleep on the sofa, his head tipped back and his mouth open as he snored slightly. She took the glass from his hand and put it on the coffee table before creeping upstairs and into his Study. She knew this was wrong, but she desperately wanted to see what it was he had been so concerned about.

There were drawers and drawers full of papers, some no more interesting than bank statements but others that she took a little more time over. She was determined to find something about the cufflinks but was distracted by a pile of letters bound by a glittering green ribbon. They were written in her mum's handwriting and she took them out of the drawer quickly and removed the ribbon, looking through them. The first one was dated a month before Rebecca's birth and the young girl read it greedily, eager to find a new connection with the mother she had lost.

Dear Gil,

Deed poll has finally come up with the goods and your child and mine will be called Williams. I hope that this means that one day I'll be able to tell it about its wonderful father and explain why things that happened over thirty years before it was born have changed what its life could have been.

You are never far from my thoughts, Gil, and I miss you more than I can write in a letter. I pray for you every night and think of you every day. Please know how much I will always love you.

All my love,

K-

Rebecca felt tears rolling down her cheeks but there were no accompanying sobs, her grief being beyond anything that sound could express. She continued to flick through the letters. The next one was a 'new baby girl' card and offered congratulations to the absent father, explaining that the baby's name would be Rebecca after her maternal grandmother, who had died two years before. There were many more, some of them just strange quotes on the back of postcards, but even they gave her the feeling of being closer to her lost mother.

Rebecca picked out one that had creases all over it from where it had been scrunched up into a ball. Curious to know why someone had wanted to get rid of it, she found herself reading on with interest.

Dear Gil,

I have changed my bank account. It seems like the only way to stop you putting money in.

I know you want to help, but it hardly seems fair that you pay towards a child you never see, through no fault of your own.

Contrary to what <u>certain people</u> believe, I didn't marry you for the money and – even if I die bankrupt – I will have come out of our short marriage with something precious: our beautiful daughter.

Rebecca is walking now. She is into everything as well! Two eyes are just not enough!

Love as always,

K-

The last letter was postmarked only three months ago, and the handwriting was wobbly and uncertain. Rebecca could imagine the pain it must have caused her mum to write the letter which was, unlike the others, more than just a note.

Dear Gil,

I'm told I have no more than a month left. It is breaking my heart to have to say goodbye to my daughter when she is only just on the cusp of becoming a young woman. I have requested that custody be granted to you but will not attend the hearings as I cannot bear it. I am not ready to let her go. Is that why I can't find the right moment to talk to her about you? I will keep trying!

Rebecca is a strong and principled girl and I could not be prouder of her. She is a city girl through and through though, and I am not sure how she will adapt to country living!

The only thing that upsets me even half as much as the prospect of losing my daughter is the fact that I will not have chance to see you again before all of this nonsense becomes reality. I sleep and dream more now (perhaps the morphine!) and in all my dreams I am back with you at Seaton and we have a family together.

Perhaps that would just make all of this harder though.

I need you to know that I think often of that day on the lake and I do not blame you. You must know this.

I lost my hair during my last round of chemo and am enclosing most of it in this letter!

This will be my last letter. Keep it with you and I promise I will watch over you with every power that is given to me.

My love for eternity,

K-

Rebecca put the letters away in the drawer and wandered slowly out of the room, trying to remember her way to her bedroom as tears were blurring her vision. She could hear her father's loud snores, and she tried to imagine him with her mum. She could not understand why her mother had kept William's identity a secret when she clearly loved him so much. There was something else troubling her, but it was not until she got to bed and was lying in the dark silence that she realised what it was.

What had her father done at the lake that required her mother to take precious time and energy to absolve him of any blame? Was it to do with the accident he had referred to earlier? She lay awake in bed for a while considering it, trying to work out what could possibly have happened to separate two people who were so much in love.

She did not remember falling asleep that night but woke up the following morning feeling prepared to meet the day head on.

It was a good thing that she was feeling strong that morning, as her father had sent off for some school prospectuses and he immediately sat her down over breakfast to discuss them with her. He was keen for her to get the best education possible but was unsure about whether or not she would respond well to the prospect of boarding.

Rebecca only half listened to him while he spoke, and she ate very little. Her mind was full of all the things she had found out since her arrival and, every time her father spoke, she got a stomach-flipping sense of déjà vu, as though she had already dreamt all the conversations she would ever have with him. On top of that, she was almost painfully disappointed that the rain would mean she could not go down to the lake and talk with Benjy.

"What do you think?" he asked suddenly, and Rebecca looked uncertain. She picked up the prospectuses and flicked through them. The annual school fees were four – or even five – figure amounts, and she could not imagine why anyone would pay such a lot to go to school. Around the writing, pictures of children, uniformly dressed and immaculately presented, smiled off the glossy pages at her. They wore designer hair accessories, jewellery or glasses and looked so pretentious – and so different from anything that Rebecca had ever seen – that she had to stop looking through them before she started laughing.

"Um, well, I don't really mind school," she said at last. "You know, normal schools. Schools full of people like me."

"How about a home tutor?"

"I'm not sure."

"You seemed to get on alright with the one I hired for you before."

"You did what?"

"When your mother was ill," William said, confused. "Terri McIntyre. You seemed to get on alright with her, I mean."

"No," Rebecca said, unable to digest all the information that had been forced upon her during the last couple of days. "The council paid for her. It's standard practice."

"The council? Is that what your mother told you? Goodness me, she really didn't want you to know about me, did she? I paid for her as soon as your mother let me know how serious her condition was."

"I want to board," Rebecca said, getting to her feet and letting her chair fall backwards. It clattered onto the old floor and she could hear it echoing behind her as she stormed out of the room, feeling angry and hurt. To make matters worse, she felt stupid for feeling the way that she did, but she could not forgive her parents for keeping so many secrets. She hated the weather for raining when she needed the freedom of going down to the lake and she hated herself for being angry with her father and especially her mum. She had always believed, and had always been led to believe, that she was the only person in her mother's life and she realised with annoyance that there was an element of jealousy in the way that she felt about her father.

She sat up in her room throughout the morning and broke her rule about talking animals, working her way through *The Wind in the Willows*, although the missing pages near the beginning made her feel slightly unsettled. When her father called her down for lunch, she was feeling better about everything and apologised for her earlier behaviour.

"I would like to go to school somewhere nearby," she told him as he set a plate of what he called 'ploughman's lunch' in front of her. "Is there a school in the village?"

"No," her father said thoughtfully, but looking far more relaxed than he had earlier. "There's a lovely little C of E primary school, but the nearest secondary school really isn't that good."

"Where did you go?"

"Eton," her father replied. Rebecca tried not to roll her eyes and instead turned the conversation back to her own choice for education.

"So, where are my options?"

"How would you feel about going to Duke of Broughley School, near Lincoln?" her father asked. "It would be a case of boarding for a week and coming home for weekends. That way you would get the best of both worlds."

Although she privately wondered what the best parts of boarding could be, Rebecca nodded. "Can we go to look around before I make any decisions?" she asked, and William nodded. They finished their lunch in silence and Rebecca enjoyed it, although she could not get rid of the taste after eating the three large, home-pickled onions, despite rushing upstairs to brush her teeth immediately after the meal.

"It's still raining," William said as she came downstairs. He was standing at the Living Room window with his hands clasped behind his back and looking out at the rain-drenched Estate. "What would you like to do?"

"Could we go into the village?" Rebecca asked. "I only went through on my way here and didn't really have chance to take it all in."

"Alright," her father said, turning around with a broad smile, "but it won't look its best in the rain."

The village was old, and as strange as Rebecca had at first thought. Her father parked the car in the marketplace and they sat for a moment looking at the rain splashing down around them. There was a large stone monument in the centre which seemed to have no purpose whatsoever, but it was cordoned off with rusting metal chains.

A Spar shop in the marketplace seemed to be doing good business, and a number of people were going in and out, carrying bags full of shopping. Many of them were pensioners, although Rebecca did not find that too surprising given that it was a weekday afternoon and most people would be at work. A couple of young mothers walked down the street together, pushing pushchairs and talking and laughing as though the rain did not bother them in the slightest. Everyone acknowledged William as they went past, and he returned the gesture by nudging the front of his deerstalker hat with his forefinger.

The houses were all made of old, red brick and many of them were roofed with a pale thatch. Her father explained that they were very traditional for that area and that, since most of them now belonged to individual families, he was surprised that they had kept the thatch. He said it encouraged spiders and other unpleasant creepy-crawlies.

The village was mainly one road which, having wound its way through the marketplace, went up to a magnificent Norman church, surrounded by a picturesque graveyard. Rebecca could hear children shouting and laughing, and William explained that the school was just the other side of the church. Whilst they were walking, the rain stopped and the sun began to shine through, causing the puddles to glisten like the crystal water on the lake. They had no oily skins with their synthetic but beautiful patterns, and Rebecca was unsure whether or not she liked their absence.

The pair went into the shop next to the church, called simply *Margaret's*, and bought themselves a homemade sausage-roll each, which was one of the most delicious things that Rebecca had ever tasted.

The church itself stood on a small but steep green mound, so that it was far and away the tallest building in the village, although she guessed that the Hall may be taller. It had a very square tower, stretching up to the heavens and harbouring a clock on each side, which chimed for the quarter of the hour. Her father led her up the church path, past a touchingly simple Celtic cross war memorial, and they went into the building through the large wooden doors.

The inside of the church was absolutely beautiful and the first thing that occurred to Rebecca was the strange red and blue glow, caused by the fact that every window was stained glass. Many of the windows depicted scenes from the Bible, a few of which she recognised, and there were others showing saints. Some of the glass must have been very old, including one which was dedicated to the memory of 'Richard Gilbert, 9th Baron Seaton'.

There was a large notice-board at the back of the church, and Rebecca smiled as she read notices from the local churchgoers. There was a 'knit-a-thon' to make jumpers and blankets for premature babies, and St Peter's – the local school – was holding a Bake Sale in a week's time to raise money for their vegetable patch at Seaton Estate.

William seemed to enjoy showing her the many references to the Gilbert family in the church. At the front, near what her father called the 'high altar', there were two rows of tombs. The effigies were rather worn and were covered in cobwebs, which Rebecca brushed away with her hand.

"Who are these?" she asked quietly. There were seven tombs in total; three men and four women.

"Your ancestors," William replied. "The oldest is Roger Philippe Gilbert. He was granted the land and title by William the Conqueror. The family legend says that Roger saved the king's life at the Battle of Hastings, but there's nothing to suggest that's true."

Rebecca smiled in awe at this almost tangible link with the history that she loved so much.

"I suppose that's his wife then?"

Her father nodded.

"So, why are there more women than men?"

"Well," William explained, "Roger's grandson, William, was married twice. His first wife died giving birth to triplets. It's very sad, really. Only one of the babies survived infancy. The other two are buried in the tomb along with her."

"Are you descended from that baby?"

"No," William said, "we're descended from his son by his second wife. The last of the triplets was a girl so couldn't inherit the Estate. She married one of the illegitimate sons of Henry I.

The family was very well thought of in those days!"

He led her back into the main part of the church, and showed her a pew at the front, which was gated off from the rest and bore the same crest that Rebecca had seen on the gates of the Estate.

"Is this our village?" she asked, struggling to take it all in.

"Historically, yes," her father smiled. "But, as I said, most of the parishioners own their own houses now. Thank goodness!"

They walked around the church a little more before William asked the inevitable. "Are you a Christian, Rebecca?"

"Kind of," she replied. "I've never really thought about it. Why, do you want me to go to church?"

"Well, I do go almost every Sunday," her father replied, "and if you would like to come at any point then it would please me greatly."

They finished looking around in silence and then walked out into the sunshine and the graveyard. The graves were all old and William explained that there was now a new cemetery at the other side of the village. The stones were quite weather-beaten, so she had to strain her eyes to make out the words that were carved into them. There were no Gilberts here, although plenty of 'faithful servants at Seaton Manor' and it seemed to Rebecca that there must have been a point in the early nineteenth century when everyone in the village was employed by the Baron at the time.

"There are none of your family here," Rebecca said, as she moved the lower branches of a yew tree out of the way to see that Belinda Frith had died a spinster in 1834, aged fifty-five years.

"There's a family plot," William said slowly. "Would you like to see it?"

Rebecca nodded and walked behind her father through the beautiful graveyard until they reached an iron gate, which looked like it had last been painted around twenty years ago and was now orange-brown with thick rust. William shuffled the latch until it came undone, and the creak that resounded as it swung open made Rebecca jump.

"It's a while since I've been in here," her father explained.

"Sacred to the memory of," Rebecca began reading from one of the stones, but it was impossible to read any more as yellow lichen had crept across it. "We should look after this place more."

"I'd like to scatter some of your mum's ashes here," William said softly. "It was one of her favourite places."

"I have mum's ashes," Rebecca replied. She walked on until she came to the gravestone of her grandparents, whose names she recognised from the newspaper article.

"Here lies the body of a beloved wife, mother and daughter Lady Margaret Anna Gilbert, 1939 to 1971, aged thirty-one. Also, of her husband, Baron Francis Richard Gilbert, 1928 to 2007, aged seventy-nine. *Requiescat in Pace*. Rest now, your souls are at peace." She paused and glanced across at William who was looking back at her thoughtfully. "That's beautiful," she whispered. "And so sad. What a long time for your dad to be a widower. No wonder it made him angry and upset."

"You're a very thoughtful thing, you know?" Her father smiled across at her with genuine warmth. She returned the gesture before her smile slipped as she looked at the next gravestone.

"Here lies the body of a beloved son and brother, Benjamin Clarence Francis Gilbert, 1959 to 1969. The boast of heraldry, the pomp of power, and all that beauty, all that wealth e'er gave, awaits alike th'inevitable hour, the paths of glory lead but to the grave. May God hold you in the palm of his hand." She stopped reading and turned to her father, tears in her eyes. "This is your brother," she whispered, realising that she had little voice.

"Yes," William replied. "My mother designed the stone and my father chose the poem. It's from a much longer one called *Elegy Written in a Country Churchyard*."

"Do you miss him?" Rebecca asked innocently, forgetting her father's discomfort about discussing his older brother. William must have known that she had forgotten for he simply nodded his head.

"In a way," he said. "But things happened that made it more difficult that anyone could ever imagine. Even my parents." He paused and looked around the graveyard before giving a slight shiver and beginning to walk away, with Rebecca following a short distance behind. She felt strange having seen the boy's gravestone and found herself imagining him lying beneath the ground, trapped in a grave with so much life left to live.

It was raining again by the time they got back to the Estate and Rebecca offered to make tea, something that her father reluctantly agreed to. She made her speciality, pizza bread, and even attempted to bake a cake but it went wrong. In the end she had to ask her father to go back into the village to get some ice-cream so that she could disguise the fact that the cake had sunk in the middle.

Alone in the house, she found her thoughts straying back to the churchyard and to the young boy who lay buried there and yet also awaited her by the lake. She wished that she was able to do something to help him, to bring him some semblance of peace as he waited for eternity.

As she walked around the Kitchen, Rebecca heard doors around the house moving slightly in a breeze that she could not feel. The creaking sound made her think of the old iron gate at the graveyard, and she wondered if it too caught this strange breeze. Her thoughts were making her feel afraid in the Kitchen but, with the strange sounds around the house, she was even more frightened of going anywhere else. Wherever she turned her head, everything would be still and orderly, but things behind her would shuffle or tremble until she spun around to look at them.

She was certain that she could hear footsteps hurrying up and down the stairs, and she found herself thinking of the many people who had lived and died in the house; masters, mistresses, children and servants. Of course, it never occurred to her that most of those whose graves she had seen earlier had lived and died in the Hall and not the Lodge. The footsteps continued, although now it sounded like one person running up and down the stairs, and Rebecca thought she could hear giddy laughter in one of the other rooms.

It was all too frightening and strange and, when at last her father arrived home, it was to find her in tears at the kitchen table. He put the ice-cream down on the worktop and sat beside her, gently putting his arms around his daughter and allowing her to cry onto his shoulder. She could not explain why she was crying, especially as she was unsure whether she had imagined the whole thing, but he did not ask her about it. He appreciated her cooking but promised that he wouldn't let her stay in the house on her own again until she was a little bit older.

"It's a big house even for two people," he said with a smile. "I've lived here alone for the last nine years or so and I still get very lonely in it."

Because of this, the following day when he met the Estate Agent at the Boat House, Rebecca went with him. The Boat House was a lovely picturesque cottage on the opposite side of the lake and not too far from the old Hunting Lodge. It was fully enclosed by a tall hedge so there was no way that her father would have seen her speaking with Benjy yesterday. It had been empty for twelve years and smelt damp and musty, but Victor Mallory, the Estate Agent, was confident that it would be snapped up quickly by the right tenant. He was particularly taken with the large room on the ground floor, which had formerly provided housing for the boat during winter.

"It would make a perfect workshop for a painter or an artisan!" he exclaimed, throwing his arms in the air enthusiastically.

After lunch, she made her excuses and headed back to the pier where Benjamin was waiting for her already.

"Have you ever been to the cemetery?" she asked, without even saying hello.

"You mean after I got my own spot there?" Benjy said. "Yes, I saw it. It was a perfect example of my mother's handiwork."

"She must have loved you very much. Were you in the house last night?" she asked, but Benjy just looked at her innocently for a moment before changing the subject.

"Did Will tell you what happened?"

"No," Rebecca said. "He would hardly talk about it."

"I wonder," the ghost said thoughtfully. "Should I tell you what happened? No, no, you wouldn't believe it even if I did tell you."

"I would!" Rebecca protested. "I trust you, Benjy. But first of all, you need to tell me if you were in the house yesterday."

"Of course not," Benjy replied. "I told you that I stay here."

Although there was something in their conversation that bothered her, Rebecca could not put her finger on what it was. So, as she was mostly satisfied with his answer, she took off her shoes and socks and dangled her legs into the water, waiting for her friend to go ahead with his story.

Eventually Benjy began, although he was obviously uncertain about telling her.

"I told you already that it was Will's seventh birthday. The cufflinks I bought him were gold with freshwater pearls. I thought it would be symbolic because we both loved going fishing."

"I read that," Rebecca said, listening intently to everything that she was being told.

"Yes. Anyway, we went out in the boat while Mother and Father entertained a few of their friends in the garden. It was the loveliest, most beautiful June day." He paused, remembering the beauty that framed his last living memories. "I was worried about the way that Will was misbehaving, shouting and screaming and such, so I said that we should stop playing on the boat. He was furious. I'd never seen him so angry, shouting 'it's my birthday' and silliness like that. He threw the cufflinks into the lake in anger and then started crying and asked me to retrieve them. I leant over to catch a hold of them, but he started rocking the boat and I fell out. I drowned because of him and he told everyone it was an accident."

Rebecca was silent. Fear and pity were choking her, and she was unable to believe that her father was a murderer.

"Still," she said, forcing the words, "he was only seven. I had a fairly bad temper when I was seven and it's easy to forget how dangerous things can be."

"Oh yes, quite," conceded the ghost. "But he tried the same trick again many years later when he took a young woman out on the boat."

"No," Rebecca gasped, remembering what her mother had written in the letter. "What did this woman look like?"

"Well, she had darker skin than you," Benjy said, trying to remember, "and she and Will seemed to be very close."

"My mum!" Rebecca gasped. "William tried to kill my mum?" Benjamin did not answer. "I can't believe she still loved him after that! And then he acted like it was his father who was to blame for her leaving."

"I should not have told you," Benjamin sighed. "I've had years to come to terms with who Will is, to accept him for himself. I do believe that he has some sickness of the mind to make him behave in that way."

"Don't give him excuses," Rebecca snapped. "I have to live with this man."

She was actually quite afraid of going back to the house, knowing as she did about her father's true nature, and she was unsure whether to mention the subject to him or not.

"No wonder he wanted to erase any trace of you in the house and can hardly bear to talk about you!" Rebecca was ranting, and she knew it. Her blood was boiling inside her. If she had felt betrayed by her parents during the last week, there was no word to describe how she felt right now.

"He would not even retrieve the cufflinks from the water," Benjamin sighed, more to himself than to Rebecca. "The one thing that would allow me to rest easily." Then he raised his voice and said firmly, "Do not go out on the boat when he is around, Rebecca. I like you too much to see you get hurt."

Rebecca agreed and hugged Benjy. He felt damp but otherwise exactly as a living boy would have done. There were rain clouds threatening and Rebecca knew that her father would soon come looking, so she hurried back to the house and spent the remainder of the day watching television and listening nervously to her father singing to himself. It was dinner before she actually saw him and, when she did, he smiled at her warmly.

"I called Duke of Broughley School and they've agreed to take us around tomorrow."

"Right," Rebecca said.

"Are you pleased?" he asked, obviously confused and, for a brief moment, Rebecca felt sorry for him. "I thought that was what you wanted?"

"Yes. Yes, of course I'm pleased," she said.

The evening was uncomfortable, and Rebecca excused herself early after dinner, saying that she wanted an early night before the busy day tomorrow. Her father did not question her decision, although he did promise to make sure that she would be up in time in the morning.

Her sleep was sporadic and disturbed as she imagined the look on William's face as he killed his only brother and tried the same with her mum, who remained dedicated to him for her short life. She was asleep, however, when her father woke her up with a knock on her door.

"Rebecca, Sweetheart, it's half past seven."

"Thanks!" she called and started to get up. As she tried to choose which pair of earrings would work best with her outfit, something Benjy had said suddenly returned to her. Retrieving the cufflinks would allow the boy to rest in peace with his parents. She smiled, determined to do that for her uncle and friend, before she went downstairs to breakfast, where her father commented on how happy and content she was looking.

"Thank you," she said. "I just seem to have got a better understanding of what I need to do." William did not ask for an explanation of her strange answer, but just smiled at her before picking up his coat and car keys and leading her outside.

Their day at Duke of Broughley School was good. Of course, Rebecca thought bitterly as they drove home, it would have been perfect if she hadn't constantly been thinking about how her father was a murderer. Every time he looked at her, he could have been thinking about doing the same to her as he had done to his ten-year-old brother.

The school itself was lovely. They were shown around by the Headmaster and the Head of one of the school's four houses. They were both helpful and enthusiastic, and she agreed to start as soon as possible. The Headmaster explained that they had a place for her to begin immediately and would she like to start the following Monday? Rebecca had said yes, she would like that a lot and, despite his crestfallen look, her father had agreed.

William insisted that they visit Lincoln Cathedral after they had looked around the school and, although she had initially resisted, Rebecca thought that it was one of the most beautiful places she had ever seen. They spent the entire afternoon looking around, but she did not feel that she had seen enough of it. Her father made an excellent tour guide, including showing her the parts of the cathedral which had featured in the *Da Vinci Code* film, which she had watched with her mum.

Following the visit, Rebecca went upstairs to her room, claiming that she had a splitting headache from the excitement of it all. Once upstairs, however, she sat on her bed and thought about how early she would need to get up to go down to the lake without her father noticing. She set her alarm for 6:30am and settled down to sleep, almost too excited as she thought of the momentous thing she would be doing tomorrow.

The morning took too long to come, and Rebecca quickly dressed and hurried down the stairs, William's snores reassuring her that the mission remained secret. She gathered everything that she might need from her father's cupboard and then strode out the door.

It was already a lovely day by the time she got outside, and she was grateful that Benjamin had another beautiful day to remember for eternity. When she got down to the lake, Benjy was waiting for her.

"I saw you coming," he explained. "What are you doing here so early?"

"I've come to find the cufflinks," she said determinedly, brandishing a small net that had obviously been bought some time ago for rock-pooling. Benjamin laughed.

"I appreciate the thought, Rebecca," he said, "but you will never find it. Anyway, Will already has one of them in a box in his Study."

"That's what he didn't want me to find!" she exclaimed. "Why don't you tell me where to fish? You can see in the water, can't you?"

"I suppose I can," Benjy said. "I had never thought of the possibility before."

Rebecca clambered into the boat and tried to manoeuvre her way across the lake, copying how she had seen people on television row. She was pleased with herself, especially as it was far harder than it looked, and she jumped when Benjamin suddenly called out to her to stop. She pulled the oars back onto the boat and, dropping the net into the water, she began fishing around but brought up nothing but weeds.

"You need to look harder," Benjy urged, sounding desperate. Rebecca nodded and peered over the edge.

Suddenly, the boat gave a lurch and Rebecca jumped to see that Benjamin was sitting opposite her. There was a maniacal grin on his usually-angelic face, and he was using his full body weight to rock the boat violently from side to side. The strange smile made him look inhuman, Rebecca thought with a stomach-churning pang of terror, and the cold stare in his eyes was like a wild animal. For a moment, their eyes locked together, and she realised that his gaze had nothing in common with her own or with her father's. He was a complete stranger to her, and she wondered what had made her go out onto the lake to help someone she didn't even know.

"Look harder," Benjy demanded, and Rebecca peered over the edge, suddenly petrified of not doing as she was told. She glimpsed across at the pier, but it was too far away for her to reach.

The boat lurched again.

"Stop it!" she cried out, panicked. "I can't keep my balance."

"Try!" Benjamin hissed, laughter evident in his voice, and gave the side of the boat a particularly heavy push with both hands. Rebecca felt herself falling and thrashed out, trying to get back to the boat but something, which felt like a hand, was holding her down in the water.

"Help!" she called. "Benjy, help!"

Although the sound of laughter continued, there was no answer. Rebecca felt a surge of determination well up inside her, and she could almost hear her mum shouting at her to swim to the edge of the lake, which was not more than ten metres from where she had fallen into the water.

Taking a deep breath, Rebecca threw all her energy into escaping from Benjy and swimming towards the pier. A thrill of relief built up in her body as she got closer and closer, remembering all the times she had argued with her mum about not wanting to take swimming lessons at primary school.

Just as she was about to stretch out to reach the edge of the lake, she felt Benjy's hand grab hold of her ankle and pull her back. Still a few metres from the safety of the pier, Rebecca felt the grip on her ankle begin to tighten, pulling her under the water. Expecting to see Benjy's face staring back at her, she looked around to see that she was caught in the bulrushes, just as her uncle had been so many years ago. Water filled her mouth faster than she could spit it out, and she continued to thrash in the lake.

"William!" she cried. "William!" The water continued to pour into her mouth and she could hear Benjy's laughter.

"Dad!" she screamed, using up all her remaining energy as she realised it was pointless to try swimming any further. She felt a strong grip on her wrist and she was pulled up onto the pier, feeling a sharp pain in her ankle as it broke free of the rushes.

Her father held her in his arms, roughly hitting her on her back and causing a considerable amount of water to emit from her mouth and nose.

She leant against his sodden shirt, breathing in the scent of men's cologne and cigarettes, which she already associated with her father. He whispered her name and, as she was losing consciousness, she felt him lifting her up and the lake disappeared into a blurry darkness.

She awoke to find herself in her father's Jaguar, wearing his wax coat over her soaked clothes. William was speeding down the Lincolnshire roads, apparently oblivious to the speed limit.

"Dad?" she whispered. "What are you doing?" She could still feel the sharp pain in her right foot, shooting up her leg, but could not immediately remember why.

"Taking you to Pilgrim's," her father replied. "What were you thinking: going out on the boat?"

"I wanted to find the cufflink for Benjy," she said softly, almost surprised to find that she was no longer concerned about hiding the truth.

"Oh, God. Like mother, like daughter," William muttered.

"What do you mean?"

"Your mother had the same obsession," he replied. "I tried to warn you that the lake was a dangerous place."

"Why did you kill your brother?" she asked, the pain making it impossible for her to keep her questions to herself or to temper them with kinder words.

"Kill Benjamin?" William gasped. "I didn't kill Benjy. He tried to kill me."

"What?"

"He threw my cufflinks into the water and told me that if I loved him I would retrieve them. Then when I tried, he rocked the boat.

113

Unfortunately for him, he fell out before I did. I was horrified. In all honesty, I probably ought to have shouted for help sooner. But my voice had just disappeared."

"Is that the truth?" Rebecca asked, remembering what William had said about parents lying to their children.

"I promise it is," he whispered, pulling into the car park. They sat in silence for a moment and then William carried his daughter into the hospital, with a little difficulty, and they sat together in the Accident and Emergency waiting room.

"Did you know about the ghost then?" she asked quietly.

"I had an idea when my father used to come back from a walk on the grounds and say he had heard someone reciting *Duck's Ditty*. It was Benjamin's favourite poem, and he and my father used to worship one another. They were so alike." William took a deep breath and put his arm around his daughter's shoulders. "I realised for certain when your mother used to sit by the lake for hours for no reason and then ask questions about things she shouldn't have known about. She became determined to find the missing cufflinks – just like you – and kept telling me it would give me closure. After the boat she was in nearly capsized and she had to swim to survive, she told me everything."

"Mum was a brilliant swimmer," Rebecca whispered. The room was becoming a blur as her consciousness began to waver again.

"She was," her father agreed. "I was amazed that she could swim so well when she was pregnant. I knew as soon as you mentioned the cufflinks that the same thing was happening again, but I just couldn't do anything to stop it. You're far too much like your mother to be banned from anything. Perhaps by trying to shield you from the lake I just made you more determined to go there."

"How did you find me today?" Rebecca whispered, but a nurse walked over to her and interrupted the conversation.

"I'm going to take you through to see a doctor now, Rebecca," she said with the broad smile that Rebecca had seen so many times from health professionals who visited her mum. It gave her no comfort or reassurance. She believed it was part of their training to master the art of beaming from ear to ear whilst giving any news, good or bad.

"Dad," Rebecca said suddenly, reaching out and taking her father's hand. She found she was not ready, after the events of the day, to be parted from the man who had saved her life. He hushed her and promised to stay with her.

The following day found Rebecca and her father together in the orchard with a picnic basket by their feet and the autumn sun on their shoulders. The orchard floor had a covering of windfall apples and William was trying to collect them all, promising to himself and his daughter that he would attempt to use them, as he had found an old cider press in the Boat House. Rebecca sat on a bench and laughed as she watched him crawling around on the floor and used her broken ankle as her excuse for not being able to help.

"A likely tale," her father muttered, simply causing her to laugh more. He had been a tower of strength for her at the hospital and she was not likely to forget his kindness. Her injury had invited all sorts of questions, which she and William had jointly answered with as much truth as possible and without mentioning ghosts or, more importantly, making her father look like an unsuitable guardian.

The trees behind her rustled slightly and she turned around, for a moment certain that Benjamin stood there, but there was nothing more substantial than the fragrant air.

"What will you do about the lake?" she asked, pulling on the coat that had been sitting unused beside her until the chill had come into the orchard.

"I've thought about that," William said, getting stiffly to his feet, "and, honestly, I don't know. I don't want to have it drained, although if I sell the Boat House then I could do. There certainly doesn't seem to be much point in having a Boat House without the lake."

"No," Rebecca whispered, "don't drain it. You've worked so hard to create the right environment for the birds and stuff."

William looked at her with a smile and put the basket of apples down on the bench beside his daughter. Then he stopped and turned around, as though he had heard something behind him. He stood there for a while looking out onto the Estate through a gap in the trees.

Rebecca thought it was better to leave him to his thoughts, so she pretended to look through the basket of apples, feeling sorry for her father. For years, he had lived with the pain of what his brother had tried to do, and then Benjamin had attempted it with the two people who William had truly cared about.

At last, William turned around. "What should we do?" he asked, and Rebecca was surprised to find that he was genuinely asking for her opinion. The only problem was that she had no idea what the answer could be.

"Is there anything that we *can* do?" she said thoughtfully. "I had thought that finding the cufflinks would help, but I suppose it isn't safe to go out on the boat." There was a silence, as they both privately acknowledged how close the previous day had come to being the most recent tragedy to happen on the lake.

William passed his daughter her crutches and then helped her to her feet. She was fiercely independent and refused his offer of help as they walked up to the Lodge together, although by the end of the walk her shoulders were painful from using the crutches.

They sat down next to each other in the Living Room and drank tea out of large mugs, which were covered with pictures of the Estate. William explained that they had been made for a school fundraiser two years previously and he had bought nearly all of them. Eventually, and perhaps inevitably, the conversation turned back to the matter of the ghost and what should be done about it.

"Would an exorcism work?" Rebecca asked, thinking of the things she had seen about the supernatural.

"Strangely enough," her father said with a smile, "there is a retired vicar in the village who was trained to perform exorcisms. It's quite incredible to hear him talk about it. But I don't know about how I would feel asking him to exorcise Benjamin's ghost. I'm sure he would privately think I'd gone mad." There was a silence in the room before he continued. "I don't suppose it would work, anyway. I think that these things only work if you believe in them and I can't say that I do, particularly."

"Me either," Rebecca conceded.

There was another silence as they both sipped their tea and racked their brains about the best way forward. It seemed strange, Rebecca thought as the silence began to feel slightly pressurised, to think that just two days ago she had believed her father to be a crazed killer and the ghostly boy to be her only friend. A part of her still felt that it was a dream, as though she would wake up and find that the past few days had never happened, and she would be safe to go down to the lake and talk with Benjy.

As though he knew what she was thinking, her father said, "Of course, it isn't safe to leave the lake as it is. If I'm not going to drain it then the boat will certainly have to go."

"Yes," Rebecca agreed. "I don't suppose even Benjamin can talk someone into wading in."

William looked at her challengingly, silently disagreeing with her statement, but said nothing.

The rest of the day was spent preparing the apples and then William ordered a takeaway, which they ate in the Dining Room. The portrait of her grandfather glared down at her and, coupled with what her father had told her, she could understand why her mum had found him to be imposing and difficult.

"Did you ever tell your dad what really happened?" Rebecca asked, picking up a spring roll with her fingers and looking at it thoughtfully.

"No," William replied. "It really wasn't worth it. It would have broken his heart, and that's assuming he believed me."

"Everything you did for years was to please him," Rebecca mused, not thinking about her words, "and he didn't care."

"I like to think he cared in his own way. He always loved Benjy, and you will know yourself that when you lose someone you love, you only remember the good points about them."

That night, Rebecca lay in bed, awake. She was sleeping in William's old room, which was now called the Guest Bedroom, as it was only up one flight of stairs and her father would be able to hear if she needed anything during the night. It was a large room, with high ceilings, and quite different from her own room in the attic. However, she was comfortable here and she was not convinced that she would be happy in the attic room, surrounded by Benjamin's things.

She was constantly being troubled by not knowing the correct thing to do. For as long as she could remember, she had enjoyed a strong conviction that there was a right way to do things and she generally knew what it was.

Now there was no such reassurance. However much her father wanted to do *something*, he did not seem to know what that something was, and Rebecca was no closer to figuring it out.

Benjamin had told her that retrieving the cufflinks would allow him to rest in peace, but she was unsure how much this was just a lie to make her go out on the boat.

At some point in the early morning, she must have fallen asleep as she woke to find the autumn sun shining through a gap in the curtains. She got up and hopped across to open them. The Estate stretched out before her like the promise of new life and hope, and she suddenly had an idea about how to lay the ghost to rest.

She picked up her crutches and hobbled downstairs to find her father reading the newspaper at the table in the Dining Room. He looked over the top of it and smiled at her as she walked in. He had laid a place for her at the opposite side of the table and, once she had sat down, he helped her shuffle the chair forward so that she was close enough to the table to eat the cereal he had put out.

"Would you come down to the lake with me today?" she asked, and laughed as her father dramatically stopped in his tracks, causing the milk he was pouring to spill over the top of her teacup.

"The lake? Why?"

"Because," Rebecca began and then stopped, feeling like an idiot. She could not expect her father to take her down to the place he hated so much – the place from which he had tried unsuccessfully to protect her and had finally been forced to come to her rescue when his fears had been realised.

"Out with it," William smiled, mopping up the spilt milk with his napkin. "I'm interested to know what could possibly make you want to go down there."

"I want to throw the cufflink into the lake."

"What?"

"The cufflink that's in your Study," Rebecca said, and William did not ask how she came to know about it. "I want to throw it back into the lake."

"Your mother – and you – nearly died retrieving that," her father said softly. "I don't think I can part with it in that way." He paused and then an enlightened look crossed his face. "I have an idea what we can do with it though. Why don't we take it up to the cemetery and bury it? Between my parents' and Benjy's graves."

Rebecca thought about it for a moment. Her father's idea seemed less dramatic; a sweet gesture rather than an act of spite or vengeance. She had imagined herself hurling the cufflink into the air and watching with a grim satisfaction as it splashed into the lake and sank down to the bottom. Now she smiled at the thought of burying it in the quiet, peaceful spot in the village, where so many people rested beneath the ground.

"Yes," she agreed. "Your idea is better."

William suggested conducting a small funeral service, akin to a marriage vow renewal ceremony, and that afternoon they went into the village and met the vicar. He was a tall, young man with a broad smile and Rebecca talked to him quite happily. He had been brought up in a similar place to her, and they talked at length about the pros and cons of country life compared to living in a pulsing city.

He did not, however, ask too many questions about why they wished to perform the ceremony. Instead he just took notes about Benjamin's short life and then talked to William a little about his parents.

"It's an unusual request," he conceded when William asked how he felt about conducting a funeral service for a cufflink. "But I have no doubt that it makes perfect sense. Sometimes we need to lay the ghosts of our pasts."

Rebecca's mouth fell open slightly at his choice of words and, although her father noticed, the vicar remained none the wiser. After they had finished the plans for the ceremony, the vicar poured himself and William a glass of brandy and handed Rebecca a bottle of *Coca Cola*. Then they sat and talked about a number of unrelated things, especially the events and politics surrounding the school – as both William and the vicar were on the Board of Governors – and the church.

When they returned to the Estate, Rebecca and her father walked down to the lake. The sun was still shining brightly but it was now quite low in the sky, so they both had to squint to see properly. As they stood there, Rebecca became absolutely certain that Benjamin was standing behind them, but William seemed unaware of any presence other than their own and the ducks', whose noisy quacking was breaking the otherwise eerie silence.

"All along the back-water," began the voice that Rebecca had heard on her first venture down to the lake. She turned around to where the voice was coming from, but it continued from a different place altogether. "Through the rushes tall. Ducks are a-dabbling."

"Up tails all!" William finished the poem with a flourish, the first sign that he had heard or seen anything of the ghost. As soon as he had spoken, Rebecca's feeling of being watched ceased and she became equally sure that they were now entirely alone. The sunlight on the lake was like a burst of crystals and she found the movement of the reeds in the wind almost hypnotic.

"If you promise to be careful," her father said, looking at her with a smile, "I'll take you up to the Hunting Lodge."

Rebecca eagerly agreed, remembering what William had said on her first day about Henry VIII using the building, and they walked around the edge of the lake, leaving the pier behind them.

The Hunting Lodge had clearly been a beautiful building once upon a time. There was a great wooden door frame made of massive, untreated tree trunks, and Rebecca could tell by looking at the remains of the door that it had once been painted red and green. Her father led her around, pointing out where it was safe to put the crutches.

"Don't go any further in," he warned and took a small black torch from his pocket. The man has everything, Rebecca thought fondly, but her loving amusement gave way to awe as she looked around.

By torchlight it held a kind of mysterious magic. The windows were boarded up, so only snatches of natural light were able to penetrate, which meant that the torch's beam was strong and golden. It lit up intricately carved beams, each with a dozen cobweb-strewn faces staring down at her. Some leered with elongated tongues protruding out of wide mouths; others smiled broadly, showing rows of wooden teeth. The cobwebs meant they all a shock of straggly silver hair, which gave Rebecca a feeling of excited terror. To her left was a mess of very old electricity wires. They had clearly been boxed up at some point, but now hung loosely down from the wall. The torch-beam dropped slightly, and she saw a large fireplace, stone and heavy, with carvings depicting men on horseback and long-legged hounds running beside them.

"It's beautiful," she gasped, feeling tears prickle her eyes at the thought of the building just wasting away.

"Yes," her father agreed. "I used to love it when I was a youngster. Of course, it wasn't quite so dilapidated then."

"When did it stop being used?" Rebecca asked, indicating to the old electrical wires.

"My great-grandfather used it, but my grandfather had it boarded up in the 1930s. He went into a lot of debt around that time after some investments failed to pay off."

"So how come you're so rich?" Rebecca asked, ignoring the bluntness of her question.

"My father may not have been an easy man, but he was certainly an intelligent one," William said with a slight smile. "He invested from a young age and made a good deal through that. Then, of course, he sold off a lot of the property after Benjamin died. That was twofold; to bring in more money but also because..." Her father trailed off.

"Because?"

"Because he didn't feel that he needed to protect the inheritance as much with his heir dead. And I'm honestly glad it worked out like that. I would rather not have so many tenants anyway."

"Is there anything that can be done to save this place?" Rebecca asked, looking around her and wiping her eyes, not an easy thing to do whilst on crutches.

"It would cost a lot," William said. "It's in a terrible state."

"I would give anything..." She stopped. She had no right to demand that her father spend his money in any particular way, and certainly had none of her own. She began to walk away, knowing that she could not bear to spend any longer in the old Hunting Lodge and imagine it falling down. William followed her and put his hand on her shoulder.

"I'll go and see the bank manager on Monday," he said gently. "Perhaps if we rent out a couple more of the cottages we'll be able to afford to do something."

Rebecca's heart leapt, not only at the thought of saving the beautiful old building, but also at the idea of having more people, perhaps even families, on the Estate. Then something occurred to her and she stopped in her tracks, looking out at the lake.

"Before we do anything," she said firmly, "we need to get rid of the boat."

They went back up to the house and, once they had enjoyed some tea, her father called the farmer and asked to borrow a tractor and trailer. The farmer promised to bring it round first thing the following morning and, when morning came, Rebecca watched her father drive off on it. He returned some time later, absolutely soaking, and left the boat on the drive in front of the house.

"We'll burn it," he shouted up to Rebecca as she limped out. "It'll be like a Viking funeral."

There was another funeral to take place first though, and the early afternoon found them both in the churchyard with the vicar. William used a trowel to dig a small hole between the two graves and, after the vicar had said a few words about Jesus and about Benjamin, William took the ornate box out of his daughter's hand and placed it in the ground.

The cufflink rattled for a moment, as though it were not stuck into the box, and Rebecca felt a shiver run down her spine. Her father put his hand gently on her arm and began to recite the poem that he had spoken at this place so many years earlier.

"All along the backwater, through the rushes tall, ducks are a- dabbling, up tails all!" The poem went on, but Rebecca was too busy looking at the rusty iron gate. She had been quite certain that people stood there but, when she tried to focus on them, they became the tall yew trees in the open graveyard beyond.

"High in the blue above swifts whirl and call – we are down a- dabbling, up tails all!" The poem came to an end, and William bent down and brushed the dirt with his hand to cover up the box. The vicar said the Lord's Prayer, and William joined in. Rebecca remembered just enough of it to mumble what she did know and make it seem as though she was reciting it with them, although her attention was still on the gate.

When they walked through, she thought she felt a slim hand run through her hair and touch her ear, not a pinch but what her mum would have called a 'tweak'. It gave her a feeling of comfort, and she smiled to herself as she followed her father to the car. They politely refused the vicar's offer of tea and went back to the Estate, where William set up the bonfire – made almost entirely of the boat and the shattered remnants of the pier – and they sat on garden chairs watching the blaze.

As her father had promised, it was like a Viking funeral, although the wet wood of the boat took a long time to catch alight and it was pitch black by the time they were able to watch it smoulder and start to burn. William's eyes glistened in the firelight, and Rebecca shuffled over to him to offer him some comfort. He put his arm around her shoulders and kissed her head. Then he lifted his hand and ran it through her hair before gently squeezing her ear between his thumb and forefinger. Rebecca jumped and pulled away.

"Oh, I'm sorry," her father said quickly. "Did I hurt you? It's stupid, I know, but it's just something that my mother used to do whenever she gave me a hug."

Rebecca shook her head but could not find any words to speak. Whether her uncle was at peace or not, she was confident that she had her grandmother's approval for what they had done that afternoon in the churchyard.

The next day they went to church together before her father collected the ashes from the bonfire and buried them in the garden. They packed what her father called a 'school trunk', although it was actually just her suitcase, then went for a drive along the twisting Lincolnshire roads. William spent the drive reminiscing about when he was a boarder, and the strange things children find amusing when they share dorm rooms. He clearly liked to talk about his school days, so Rebecca just sat quietly in the front seat and enjoyed his company more than his stories.

That night, they sat in the Living Room together and William lit a fire, which seemed tame after the magnificence of yesterday's bonfire. As they were sitting together, Rebecca again asked her father what had alerted him to her predicament on the lake earlier in the week. William looked at her for a second and narrowed his eyes as though he was weighing her up.

"I woke up to the smell of perfume," he said at last.

"I wasn't wearing perfume."

"It was *Charlie Gold*," William said softly. Rebecca stared at him.

"Mum's perfume."

"Yes," her father nodded. "I must have dreamt about her and associated the smell or something, but it seemed very real. I went up to your room to see you and realised you were gone. The rest, as I've told you, I had already worked out."

There was a silence for a few minutes as Rebecca thought about what her father had told her. Then, in a voice smaller than she thought was possible, she whispered, "Dad, do you think that Mum's looking after me?"

"Undoubtedly," William said, and put his hand gently on her arm, his eyes once again shining in the firelight.

The following morning, they left the Lodge early and her father drove her to school. It had taken her a long time to get ready in the morning with the ridiculous cast on her leg, and she refused to have her first day at school looking anything less than her best. Their journey took them through several little Lincolnshire villages – although none of them were as pretty as Seaton – and along a road that her father called 'Ermine Street' which, he explained to her, was a Roman road built to join London to Lincoln and York.

After about an hour, they arrived. They were met just inside the building by the headmaster, who expressed concern regarding Rebecca's ankle but was clearly eager to ensure that she would settle in immediately.

"I should probably go," William said as someone came to take Rebecca's bags to the dormitory. He put his arms around his daughter and kissed her on the cheek. "I'll see you on Friday. Hopefully I'll have some news then about what we can do with the Hunting Lodge."

"Thanks, Dad," she whispered and held him as tightly as she could. Once they had separated, the Headmaster, who had been hanging back slightly, directed his newest pupil to her first classroom and she turned to go.

"Remember," William called after her, and she turned around to see a mischievous glint in his penetrating eyes, "no boating."

"Don't worry, I won't," Rebecca replied with a laugh, and walked down the corridor.

She joined with a number of other pupils and, for the first time in a year, she felt completely at ease. Here, she was not the child whose mother was ill, or dying, or dead. Nor was she in care, nor living with a stranger, and the ghostly boy at the lake could not touch or harm her. In this school, she realised, she was just another pupil – albeit a new pupil – and her fears and background were only as prevalent as she made them.

She smiled as she looked down at her timetable to discover that her first subject on a Monday morning was History.

Also by **CROWVUS**

Child of the Isle

Follow Susan's story through her memories of rural and village life in the post-war era, when the past and future ways of life were colliding.

£7.99

Day's Dying Glory

Share the adventures of three sisters living in Highland Scotland during the Napoleonic Wars.

£9.99

www.crowvus.com

www.judithcrow.co.uk

Lightning Source UK Ltd.
Milton Keynes UK
UKHW021917021118
331673UK00003B/21/P